HOTBED HONEY
Toni Blake

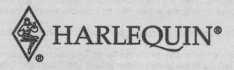

HARLEQUIN®

TORONTO • NEW YORK • LONDON
AMSTERDAM • PARIS • SYDNEY • HAMBURG
STOCKHOLM • ATHENS • TOKYO • MILAN • MADRID
PRAGUE • WARSAW • BUDAPEST • AUCKLAND

To Joni Lang,
my friend, fellow writer and frequent partner in crime,
who once shoved a couple of Harlequin Temptation
novels into my hand and said,
"You should try writing romance."

ISBN 0-373-25900-X

HOTBED HONEY

Copyright © 2000 by Toni Herzog.

This edition published by arrangement with Harlequin Books S.A.

Visit us at www.eHarlequin.com

Printed in U.S.A.

"Is that what you brought to sleep in?"

Kimberly bit her lip and forced herself to look at Max, who was already in bed. "Well, I didn't think ratty pajamas would really fit my new image. You said before that it was possible Carlo might sneak around in the night. I thought he might see me."

"*Too* much of you."

Max's eyes were still on her, as if glued to her.

"You sound jealous, Tate," she murmured, as she climbed into bed.

"Don't be ludicrous. And the idea is to be friendly to the guy, Brandt, not incite him to attack you."

Max reached up and flipped the switch that darkened the room. He desperately wanted to roll over and touch her. It would be easy, so *easy*…. The lust he felt for her was intense. If he stayed in this bed much longer, he'd be reaching out beneath the sheets and…

Damn it! Max couldn't sleep here and not have her. Grabbing his pillow, he made his way to one of the overstuffed easy chairs across the room.

It would be a very long night….

Dear Reader,

I still remember the day I decided to be a writer. I announced it to my mother over breakfast at the age of ten, then proceeded to write my first novel—nineteen notebook pages long. A lot has changed since then, but my dream of being a novelist never wavered. So it is a dream come true to present you with my first Harlequin Temptation novel.

When the characters of Max Tate and Kimberly Brandt first came to life in my head and then on my computer screen, I didn't realize how sexy this book would become. But Max and Kimberly share a tumultuous history, and when they are forced back into each other's lives, all the old issues, and old *passions*, become new again. For me, their story is about forgiveness and redemption, the depth of a rekindled desire and learning to accept the people we love— complete with their flaws.

I hope you enjoy reading *Hotbed Honey* as much as I enjoyed writing it. Please visit me on the Web at http://www.toniblake.com.

Sincerely,

Toni Blake

1

"I NEED A WOMAN."

"Don't we all."

"I don't need a woman for *that*," Max Tate said, casting a dry look at Frank Marsallis. He took a sip of the Scotch Frank had just shoved into his hand. "If I want *that*, I can get it. I need a partner for a job."

Frank lifted one stubby finger in the air as he gave a somber nod. "Aha. I should've known you weren't here just to crash my party."

Standing in Frank's lavish entryway, Max took an absent look across the expansive area that his onetime mentor called a "living room." Stylish-looking people stood in clusters drinking and talking as a slow, bluesy tune cascaded from speakers hidden in the vaulted ceiling. Not really his kind of scene, or at least not by choice. All things considered, he'd rather be drinking a beer in a neighborhood bar. Especially considering the way he looked at the moment. "Crashing parties isn't my style, Frank. Anyway, the job starts tomorrow morning."

Frank rolled his eyes, letting his blue gaze land on his fellow P.I. "Nothing like waiting till the last minute, Max."

Max didn't have time to deal with Frank's annoyance. "Look, I've been busy with a job that went longer than planned. Can you help me or not?"

"One question first. Why do you look like you've been living in a trash can?"

"Like I said, I've been busy. I just came from doing a little undercover work." Undercover assignments were Max's specialty.

"As what?"

"A garbageman." He slanted Frank a look of warning. "And no cracks, please—I don't have time for your wit right now. I need to know if you can get me the woman."

"All right," Frank said, offering a highly exaggerated sigh. "What are the parameters?"

"She needs to be quick-thinking," Max told him, glad to get down to business. "And she has to have good instincts. She should also be a good actress."

"Anything else?"

Max snapped his fingers. He'd almost forgotten the most important part. "Yeah. She has to be drop-dead gorgeous."

Frank shook his graying head in clear irritation, then returned to the matter at hand. "All right, why do you need a good actress?"

"She's going to pretend to be my wife."

"And why does she have to be gorgeous?"

"Same reason."

Frank cast him yet another cutting look, but this time Max turned a sly grin toward his friend.

"Actually, the job calls for it, Frank, in a big way. The guy I'm trying to nail only goes after really hot women."

Frank took the last sip of his drink and set his glass on a nearby table. "So this means she'll be bait."

Max knew Frank didn't like the sound of that, but it was often the nature of the business for women who chose this line of work. "Something like that. That's where the quick thinking and good instincts come in. Besides, I'll be there the whole time, either out in the open or in hiding, keeping an eye on things."

Frank sighed again, then scanned the room while Max waited impatiently. If Frank couldn't come through for him on this, he was sunk. In between stints of playing garbageman, he'd spent the last two weeks drawing Carlo Coletti into this scheme, and he'd made it clear to Carlo that not only was he loaded, but that he had a beautiful wife to shower his riches on. Without one, the whole case would flop. And Frank was the only guy in town he trusted enough to "borrow" another P.I. from. He knew from experience that Frank hired only the best.

Frank's head suddenly darted around to face him. "I thought you were quitting." It sounded suspiciously like an accusation.

Max tilted his head derisively. "Not quitting, Frank. Stepping back. Growing the business. Bringing in some new blood."

"Quitting," Frank repeated.

Well, so what if he was? Max thought. He'd been in this business up to his ears for fifteen years, since he was twenty years old, for God's sake. He'd had his own firm for the last three of those years, and now he finally had the money to hire enough good people so that he could get out of the field himself. He liked the work and was damn good at it, but he'd fallen into it by chance all those years ago. He and Frank had met through a mutual friend, which had resulted in an unexpected job offer at a time when Max had been looking for some direction in life. Well, he'd ended up with a definite direction, all right, but now wanted to see what it was like to have a job where he didn't risk his life every single day. So he planned to manage the P.I.'s he'd soon hire, be the brains behind the operation and let someone else be the brawn—and the garbagemen— for a change.

"Anyway," Max said, "I just finished up the garbage gig, so this next one is my last case. Worth a fortune if I can pull it off. But like I said, I need a woman. Do you have one for me?"

Frank gestured across the room. "See the brunette in the blue dress?"

Max followed Frank's gaze. Did he ever. She stood with her back to them, talking with another woman as they studied an impressionist print that hung above Frank's fireplace. She had legs that went on forever, dark brown silky hair that fell in waves to her shoulders and a nice shape inside that dress to back it all up.

Even without seeing her face, Max knew she was a beauty, just what he was looking for. So he didn't hesitate. He looked at Frank and winked. "I'll take her."

"OKAY, KIM, this is the place. Number 230. Go on in and introduce yourself. I'll park the car and join you in a minute."

Kimberly Brandt stepped out of Frank's mint-condition 1977 gold Cadillac into the lightly falling rain. She slammed the door, blotting out the sounds of

B. B. King, and hurried up the front steps of the stylish condo.

She rang the doorbell and waited, realizing that she didn't even know the guy's name. All she knew was that Frank had volunteered her to be the guy's wife for a few days, which sounded a bit complicated, but interesting, too. She'd done plenty of undercover work in the past, but since joining Frank's agency a year ago, she usually worked alone. This might be a challenging change. Maybe even fun. And good training for cases that required a team approach.

She rang the doorbell again and pulled the thin, beaded shawl she wore tighter around her as the rain began to seep in. *Come on, buddy. Answer the door.*

Frank had also told her she was going to be used as bait for a thief who liked to seduce his victims before robbing them. That part *wouldn't* be so fun, but she knew she could handle it. She'd gotten quite good at her job over the past few years.

"Damn it," she muttered, pressing the doorbell once more, holding it for a few seconds this time. She could be a tough chick when she needed to be, but she didn't like standing out in the rain for no good reason. If she didn't get inside soon, her rayon dress would just be one big wad of crinkles.

She glanced up and down the rain-slickened sidewalk, irritated. Where was Frank? Was this guy even home? According to Frank, he'd headed here to get cleaned up after an undercover operation, but where was he? If it was such an emergency to meet tonight, why wasn't he opening his door and welcoming her with open arms?

On impulse, she reached down and twisted the doorknob.

The door was unlocked.

More surprised than she'd expected, she let go and watched the door ease to a stop after opening halfway. She'd only turned the knob for the hell of it—she hadn't thought it would actually get her inside. *What a bozo, not even keeping his door locked. Well. What now?*

"Hello?" she called, leaning through the doorway. No answer. But there were lights on and music playing low but potent. Pearl Jam. *"Hello?"* she yelled again.

"I'm with Frank Marsallis, and I'm getting soaked out here," she said, trying to project her voice as she tentatively placed one foot over the threshold. "So I'm coming inside now."

Standing in the sunken entryway of a dimly lit living room, she suddenly thought, *God, please let this be the right condo.*

"Julie, is that you?" a deep male voice called.

Julie? Hardly. Maybe this *was* the wrong condo. "Um, no, not Julie," she answered. "I'm here with Frank Marsallis."

She'd barely uttered the last sentence when a man turned the corner at the top of the small flight of stairs, wearing nothing but a hunter-green towel around his waist. The first thing she noticed was that he had a great body, rife with nice, medium-size muscles, which were her favorite kind. The second thing she noticed was that he was...*Max!*

Max, whom she hadn't seen since the Carpenter case three years ago. Max, who was just as excruciatingly handsome as ever.

Their eyes met and held. Kimberly's heartbeat increased with all the conflicting memories of him that raced through her brain. It took a lot of effort, but she finally forced her mouth to close. Then she swallowed, hard.

"Oh no," Max said, shaking his head. "Oh-h-ho no. This can't be. It just can't. Please tell me *you're* not the woman Frank sent me." He was laughing now, but not in a happy way, more like a delirious, he-couldn't-believe-his-rotten-luck kind of way.

Which made her feel lousy, but didn't surprise her. She might have loved the guy once, but that didn't mean she was any happier to see him at the moment than he was to see her. "As a matter of fact, I am."

"This is my worst nightmare," he muttered as he came down the stairs.

Oh, so this was how it was going to be, huh? She glared at him. "You're not exactly my first choice of a partner, either," she snapped. "Or my second. Or my tenth."

He raised his eyebrows. "*You're* complaining about working with *me*? I don't believe this!"

"Well, believe it. When did you get back to L.A., anyway?"

"About six months ago."

She narrowed her gaze and tilted her head. "And here I thought I'd never have to see you again. What on earth brought you back?"

He returned her condescending tone. "There aren't enough good P.I. firms in this town. And I figured enough time had passed since you ruined my reputation that I could come back and open up shop here."

She sucked in her breath at the accusation. How dare

he! "Ruined? *Ruined?* One little incident and you
blame me for—"

"All right, what the hell's going on in here?" The
booming sound forced both Kimberly and Max to shift
their gazes to Frank, whose heavyset frame filled the
doorway, his eyes wide and his coat soaking wet. "I
could hear you two all the way out on the street. And
Max...what are you doing parading around in a
towel?"

"Frank, you've gotta get me another woman."

"What's wrong with this one?" Frank motioned to
Kimberly with outstretched hands.

"*This one* has a habit of tipping off my suspects."

"What?" Frank asked, confusion in his eyes. "She's a
good P.I., Max. And the only suitable one I've got at the
moment. She'll have to do."

"*She,*" Kimberly interjected, planting her fists on her
hips, "is not a cut of meat on a slab, gentlemen. She's
standing right here, so maybe you could quit address-
ing her in the third person."

Max looked at her. "You just did the same thing
yourself."

She rolled her eyes. "For effect. See how annoying it
sounds?"

"I still don't know why you're not wearing any
clothes," Frank pointed out.

"I was in the shower," Max said, "and she came in
without knocking. It might be one thing if I were an
elusive suspect, but—"

"I rang the bell three times!"

Max ignored her and looked back to Frank, eyes
pleading. "Come on, Frank. Get me somebody else.
Anybody else."

"I told you, there *is* nobody else. I only have two other women who fit the bill, and they're already in the middle of other cases." Frank took a step toward Max. "Look, Kim will do a good job for you—she's never let me down."

Max eyed her critically and she knew he was remembering it again—the Carpenter case. She wanted to cringe, but instead she just kept scowling at him. She was a much better P.I. than he'd ever given her credit for and she wouldn't let herself be cowed into guilt or submission by his accusing look.

"Never let you down, huh?" Max said, sounding as if he didn't believe a word of it.

"No, she hasn't. Now, how do you two know each other, anyway?"

Max held his gaze on her. "We used to work together."

She didn't look away. "But then we got fired."

"Because *she* tipped off an embezzler that we were on to her," he clarified, accusation in his voice.

"An incident which I've never had the opportunity to give my version of."

But Max was shaking his head and she could see that he still wasn't interested in her side of the story, even three years later. She'd be damned if she was going to waste her time trying to make him listen. "Look, do you want me for the job or not, Tate?"

He sighed, muttering beneath his breath. "Talk about being between a rock and a hard place."

"Believe me, this is hardly my dream scenario, either. But I'm a professional and I can handle it. If *you* can't," she challenged, "say so, and I'll happily be on my way."

She waited for his answer, her heart in her throat. She didn't know why. Or maybe she did. It was more than a little surprising to her, but maybe she really wanted this now, suddenly, the chance to work with him again, the chance to clear her name with him. Maybe she really wanted to show the pompous, arrogant jerk just how good she was, once and for all. She'd never thought she'd have the chance to do that, but now, here it was, dropped in her lap like some unexpected gift.

Still, Max said nothing, and she wasn't about to beg or even let him know she had anything to gain by this at all. So after waiting for what she decided was a reasonable length of time, she turned to leave. Working with him would only be torture anyway. "Come on, Frank. Let's go back to your party. Maybe there are still some hors d'oeuvres left."

"Wait." The voice came from Max, and it made her chest tighten in some combination of victory and nervousness. The old adage came back to her, Be careful what you wish for. Nonetheless, she smiled inside at the idea of making him crumble by threatening to leave. It was good to see Max squirm a little, and although she knew most people wouldn't consider this squirming, she also knew it was as close as Max would ever come.

She slowly turned and looked up at him. "Yes?"

His words sounded almost wracked with pain. "All right. Come on in and I'll...brief you about the case."

Her heartbeat increased again, but she didn't smile, in favor of looking regally triumphant. "Go back to the party, Frank," she told her boss. "I can handle things from here."

He raised his eyebrows. "Sure you two won't claw each other's eyes out as soon as I walk out the door?"

Kimberly slanted a look in Max's direction. "A tempting notion, but I'll try to resist."

Frank looked hesitant. And with good reason, Kimberly thought. For all he knew, she and Max *would* kill each other. But, shaking his head, Frank departed, pulling the door shut behind him and closing out the gentle sounds of falling rain that had become more audible since Kimberly and Max had stopped yelling.

So now they were alone. Everything was quiet, except for the low murmur of music from the stereo, which Max walked over to and turned off, immersing them in total and intense silence.

He looked back at Kimberly, who still stood in the foyer, and held her gaze once more. She wished she could read his eyes, but she'd never gotten very good at it. Still, looking into them reminded her of something she hadn't expected, something that caught her totally off guard—how much she'd *loved* those eyes once upon a time. They were a warm, wrap-around-you shade of brown. And sometimes, she recalled, they were more than warm, they were hot. *Very* hot. Like when the two of them were moaning in a glorious symphony of sex.

Uh-oh, she hadn't meant to start thinking about that stuff. She shifted her weight from one foot to the other and glanced toward the floor.

"Come in and sit down and I'll, uh...go put some clothes on," he said.

"Good idea." In fact, it was the best idea she'd heard since walking through Max Tate's door. The sight of his body had obviously started rekindling some old fires inside her and that wasn't good. For one thing, they were enemies and she refused to let herself be attracted to him after the way things had ended between them. And for another, they were about to be partners in a potentially dangerous case, which would require all her concentration. So she promised herself that she simply wouldn't think about the sexual aspect of what they'd once shared. She'd blot it right out of her mind. It was the only sensible way to handle the situation.

And now that she had *that* little misunderstanding cleared up with herself, she could think about this case and what suddenly made it so important to her on a *personal* level. She needed to prove to Max Tate that she was a good P.I.

After he'd gone, Kimberly climbed the few stairs to the living area and settled on the leather sofa pushed against the back wall of the spacious, high-ceilinged room. As she straightened her dress, she looked around and saw...his life. His life without her. Okay, so thinking about why the case was important to her wasn't all that easy at the moment. Her eyes were drawn to pictures on the small marble mantel, frames around people that weren't her. Prints on the wall that he hadn't owned when she and Max had been dating. Magazines on the table that she'd never known him to have an interest in before. In fact, even the furniture was new.

So, apparently everything had changed for Max. He'd packed up, gone to Las Vegas, and come back a new man. But it was clear that one thing *hadn't* changed. He still hadn't forgiven her for what had happened on the Carpenter case. Kimberly's stomach clenched with the memory and she strengthened her vow to prove to him that she could do her job and do it well.

She looked around Max's living room again, and then it hit her in a whole new, powerful, horrible way. Oh God, she was really going to be working with Max again. Max, who had been so much more than just a lover to her, whether or not he knew it. Max, whom she'd wanted to build a life with and wake up next to every morning until they were old and gray. This had been about the last blow she'd expected today.

But she was an adult. And a professional. She'd told Max she could handle it, so what choice did she have now?

She only hoped she didn't do anything to mess up his career again. And she hoped that she didn't somehow end up falling into bed with him again, which seemed pretty unlikely considering how much he seemed to despise her. But stranger things had happened and...oh brother, what had she just gotten herself into?

MAX LET the towel drop at his feet. He went to the chest of drawers and pulled out a pair of gray boxer briefs, stepping into them. Then he yanked a pair of worn blue jeans up from the bedroom floor and put them on, using one hand to swipe a lock of still-wet hair up off his forehead.

He caught a glimpse of himself in the mirror above the dresser as he passed by. It made him come back to reality and quit going through the hurried motions of putting on clothes and getting ready to brief his partner.

This wasn't just another case. And he wasn't getting dressed to meet with just another partner.

Kimberly Brandt was sitting in his living room. *Kimberly Brandt* was about to be his partner on the last case of his career.

He rolled his gaze heavenward and sighed. "What could I *possibly* have done to deserve this?"

Hell, he probably should have let her leave with Frank when she wanted to. This was a bad idea, there was just too much bad blood between them to pull this off. But as he'd told Frank earlier, he'd really had no choice in the matter. He needed a female partner and he needed her by tomorrow morning.

Still, for the first time since he'd taken this case, he began to feel a niggling sense of doubt and worry. Mistrust. The same mistrust that he'd had after the Carpenter case. The same mistrust that had made him choose to run his business as a one-man operation when he'd moved to Vegas. If you didn't make the mistake of depending upon other people, they couldn't mess things up for you.

Leaving the West Coast and starting over, opening his own firm, had been the best thing Max had ever done. No one knew him in Vegas or knew what had happened. He'd performed at peak level for the entire two and a half years he was there. And he'd discovered that when the gambling mecca's high rollers needed a private investigator, they were more than willing to loosen their purse strings.

He'd made a killing in just two years...but he'd also gotten tired. He'd finally admitted to himself that he just didn't like living in the neon desert. So he'd come home with a plan to establish his firm in L.A., but this time to hire enough good P.I.'s that he could get out of the field.

And now...now he had to worry about this assignment turning into another Carpenter case. It could ruin his career all over again. His chest tightened at the thought.

On another rainy night three years ago he'd had an appointment with Margaret Carpenter, a white-haired old woman who walked with a cane and always carried her silver poodle, Lacey, in her free arm. He knew this because he'd been watching her through surveillance equipment in a van parked outside her house for over three weeks. Only, Margaret Carpenter hadn't been there when he'd arrived that night. She'd packed up everything, including her dog and her stolen money, and hadn't been seen since. And it had been all Kimberly's fault.

He and Kimberly had both been working for the Kessler Agency at the time, the biggest and most prestigious P.I. firm in the city. He'd been at the company for nearly ten years and had gradually worked his way up to being assistant V.P. He'd hired Kimberly with no experience because she'd seemed so eager and earnest and so willing to learn. He'd had no idea they would soon start dating.

But date they did, heavily. And it had been going well. Yet four months into the relationship and six months into Kimberly's employment, Margaret Carpenter had come along.

It had been a pretty simple case initially. Margaret Carpenter's son, Bruce, believed his mother had been stealing money from his business and he'd hired Kessler to prove it. The first angle Max took involved sending Kimberly in as a new neighbor. He set her up in a small bungalow next to Margaret's little house and Kimberly forged a relationship with her. Kimberly kept a tiny tape recorder on her through all their visits, the idea being simply to get Margaret to confess, and hopefully to confess how she'd done it, as well, so that they could track down the physical evidence.

Max should have known there was trouble when Kimberly told him she'd met Bruce Carpenter, when he stopped by his mother's house one day. She'd found him rude and brutish. "He's just plain mean to her, Max," she'd said.

"Of course he's mean to her," Max had replied. "He knows she's embezzling his profits."

Kimberly succeeded in getting Margaret to admit to her that she had over a hundred thousand dollars hidden away and that she was looking for a good investment, but she never told Kimberly where she'd gotten the money. Still, it had been pretty obvious—she didn't work, lived meagerly, and had access to her son's accounts, a mistake of him being too trusting when he opened his construction business some years before.

The next angle they planned to take was to send Max in as a friend of Kimberly's, a real-estate broker who could help Margaret invest her money. He would ask her how much money she had and tell her he needed more, quickly, for the investment. Even if they couldn't get a confession from her, they'd watch the accounts for the amount Max requested.

But by the time Max got there that night, the house was dark and Margaret Carpenter was on her way into hiding. Unbeknownst to him, Kimberly had broken all the rules of ethics by telling Margaret who they were and what her son suspected.

He remembered all too clearly the day he and Kimberly had both been called into Dean Kessler's office. Max had found out Kimberly was responsible for Margaret's departure just moments before. She'd told him herself, obviously sensing why Kessler had requested a meeting with them both.

Kessler had first fired Kimberly, after berating her and explaining to her that they all could have lost their licenses over this kind of unethical behavior.

And then Kessler had fired Max.

Max hadn't seen it coming because he'd thought he was only involved as Kimberly's direct superior. Instead, Kessler had held him completely accountable for Kimberly's bad decisions. "You hired her and you put her on this case. You also got sloppy, Max."

"Sloppy?" He'd leaned forward and raised his eyebrows.

"This is what happens when you start thinking more about your employee's skirt than her work. You lose your judgment and she botches the job."

When he was finished, Kessler simply walked out of his office, leaving them both alone. Max sat back in the big leather chair he occupied, contemplating the reality that he'd just lost his job, his career, everything he'd worked to build for the previous ten years. He was dumbfounded—and furious—that it could be taken from him that quickly.

Slowly, he turned his head to look at Kimberly, the woman he had trusted. Tears stained her cheeks as their eyes met. Her voice was barely a whisper. "I suppose it's too late to say I'm sorry."

Sorry? He'd just lost his whole career! Sorry seemed a meaningless word in that devastating moment. "Too late," he finally said. "And too little."

She'd swallowed visibly and they'd simply stared at each other for a very long moment. Then she'd gotten up and walked away. Out of the office. And out of his life.

He hadn't seen her again until he'd exited the shower twenty minutes ago and found her standing in his foyer, rainwater dripping from the hem of her short blue dress and the tips of her wavy hair, a smug sassiness he didn't remember from before overflowing from her. She was everything he'd asked Frank for. Smart. A decent actress. And God knew, she was a pleasure to look at.

But there'd been one thing he'd left out of his description of the perfect lady partner when he'd talked to Frank. Trustworthiness. She'd proven to him three years ago that she couldn't be counted on to maintain her loyalty or to finish a job. She'd cost him everything.

And now they were supposed to work together?

KIMBERLY CROSSED and uncrossed her legs. Then she firmly crossed her arms under her breasts. What the hell was taking him so long? First he'd kept her waiting at the door, now in his living room. How long did it take a man to get dressed?

Finally, she released a sharp sigh of disgust and leaned forward on the couch. "Um, excuse me in there?" she yelled. "Those clothes you went to put on? Are you weaving the fabric yourself or...?"

When he exited the bedroom and walked toward her down the hardwood hall in bare feet, she flinched. His chest was also bare, and his jeans were pleasantly snug. Oh my. She leaned back into the couch and tried to pretend she hadn't just had a spasm at the very sight of him.

"You bellowed?" he asked, widening his warm eyes in a way that might have struck her as innocent if she hadn't known he was taunting her with them.

"I just wanted to make sure you hadn't dozed off or something." She answered, fidgeting. "And if this is going to take a while, shouldn't you call Julie and change your plans?" Oh drat. She'd tried to resist saying that last part, but it hadn't worked. Despite herself, she wanted to know who Julie was.

But all she got for her efforts was yet another of Max's classic dry looks as he shoved a lock of midnight-colored hair from his forehead. "Don't worry, Brandt. I'm completely capable of handling my own affairs."

The response cut Kimberly to the quick. Although she didn't know what bothered her more—the allusion she knew he was making to the Carpenter case and his opinion that she wasn't capable of handling *anything*, or hearing him say the word *affairs* and thinking of him having them, not with her anymore, but with other women. With this, this Julie person.

However, Kimberly quickly decided it must be the former that ate at her the most. She had the compulsion, just one more time, to try to explain to him why she'd done what she'd done that night. "Believe it or not, Tate, I'm capable, too. More than capable. And as for the Carpenter case—"

He held up his hand. "Stop."

She leaned forward and snapped her response. "Why?"

He settled in a leather chair across from her. "Because if this is going to work, you and I are going to have to push our bad feelings for each other aside and stick to the case."

"That's a spiffy plan, Tate, but if you'd just let me tell you my side of things, I'm sure we'd both—"

He cut her off. "Nope. The past is in the past and I, for one, have no desire to dredge it up. That's how it has to be if we're going to work together."

She released a bitter sigh. She should have known better. After all, she'd tried to explain her actions outside Kessler's office that day, but he hadn't let her. He'd just kept saying, "You told her *what?*" and glaring at her with disbelieving eyes. Then Kessler had called them in and that had been the end of it. He wouldn't let her explain then, and he wouldn't let her explain now. "Fine," she bit off.

"Now, about the case."

She shifted on the couch and tried to relax a little, tried to adapt a professional frame of mind. "I'm listening."

"The guy we're after is Carlo Coletti. Carlo has a pastime of robbing wealthy wives of their expensive jewelry."

"How does he go about it?"

"He hangs out in upper-class drinking establishments until he can befriend some rich guy and cling to him. He makes a point of getting the husband to show him a picture of his wife, who, as far as I can tell, has to be a knockout in order to get Coletti interested. Then he ingratiates himself into the couple's lives. After that, he seduces the wife and steals her jewelry in the process."

Kimberly tilted her head. He'd obviously glossed over some details. "Fill in the gaps, Tate."

"Well," he sighed, "in my client's case, Carlo seduced her and at the same time managed to charm the jewelry away from her. Told her it turned him on to make love to a woman decked out in diamonds. She went to her safe, put on every diamond necklace and bracelet she owned, slept with the guy, then woke up hours later naked of even the jewels."

Kimberly was beginning to think she got the picture here. "So, it's more than just money for this guy. He's after the thrills, too."

Max gave a short nod. "Would seem that way. Another thing that points in that direction is the fact that he could just pick up rich *single* women. But he only goes for couples. He seems to enjoy seducing the gorgeous wife away from her wealthy husband. That's why the scam tears the victims apart. In addition to robbing my client, Carlo broke up her marriage in the process."

"You said *victims*. There are others besides this woman?"

"I've talked with four."

"Max, if everyone knows what happened, and if this guy is so easy to find, why isn't he behind bars?"

He offered her a wry smile. "That's the tricky part. Police have checked him out, held him on suspicion— he even went to trial once. But he says he didn't do it and no one can prove anything. The most frustrating part is that he *admits* he seduces the wives, but that's it. No jewelry. To top it off, the guy lives in a dumpy apartment near Venice, west of Lincoln Avenue. It's been searched over and over and the police never turn up anything. The most valuable things this guy has in his possession are his car and the clothes on his back, which make him fit in with the rich set at a glance. But whatever he's doing with the jewelry, he's covering his tracks and keeping it quiet. He's stolen over three million dollars' worth of jewels from the four women I've spoken to, yet there's not a shred of evidence."

"And that's where we come in."

"Right. Tomorrow morning you and I will move into a mansion in Beverly Hills, borrowed from an uppercrust friend of my client's, a studio bigwig who's out of town for the next month. Tomorrow night, Carlo Coletti joins us for dinner, I'll invite him to spend the night and the party begins."

Kimberly crossed her arms over her chest. "One question. If you didn't even know who your wife was going to be, you obviously couldn't show the jerk her picture. How'd you reel him in without it?"

Their eyes met. "I assured him that my wife was the most beautiful, sexy woman he'd ever have the pleasure of meeting."

Is she? Kimberly instantly wanted to ask. His gaze and those words made her throat tighten and the juncture between her thighs tingle. She rose from the couch, suddenly anxious to end the meeting. "So then, is there anything else I need to know?"

He stood up, as well. "Nothing I can't fill you in on tomorrow. But be prepared—the guy's gonna be all over you as soon as he gets one look. And if you have any sexy clothes, bring them. We want to paint you as...not unwilling."

"Sexy clothes," she murmured, unable to think because she was still stuck on the first thing he'd said—*The guy's gonna be all over you.* Wrong guy, she thought longingly. Then she cursed herself. *Damn it, quit thinking about Max like that.*

"Something like what you're wearing right now," he added.

It took her a second to realize that he was referring to sexy clothes. She looked down, unaware that the simple blue sheath qualified. "This?"

He nodded. "I saw you from the back at Frank's party. Even without seeing your face, you were easily the hottest woman in the room."

Despite the suggestive words, his voice held zero emotion. So Kimberly turned away when she felt the warmth of a blush assault her cheeks. She padded across the floor toward the mantel and studied the photos in an attempt to block out the fluttering sensations that rippled through her body. Which one might be Julie? A closer look revealed that none of them could be. She saw two pictures of his parents—an older one and another more recent—and a picture of Max and his three brothers taken long before she'd known him. Still, the exercise hadn't succeeded in distracting her enough. Every part of her body remained completely aware of his presence and what he'd just said.

"I'll get you a cab," Max announced behind her, but she still didn't turn around. She didn't want him to see how his words had affected her, although she kept hearing them over and over again.

A few long minutes later, the beep of a horn outside announced the taxi's arrival, something that Kimberly more than welcomed. She grabbed her purse and shawl, then moved briskly to Max's front door, whisking it open to admit the sound of the rain and a glimpse of the shiny black street.

"Give some thought to your part and establish a character," he told her before she exited.

She turned to peer back up at him, unable to resist a last glance at the man she'd thought she'd never see again. Her heart ached a bit at the sight of him, and at the memories of what they'd once had.

"I'll be by to pick you up at ten tomorrow morning," he told her. "After that, we'll be as good as married."

2

IT WAS STRANGE to be driving to Kimberly's apartment after all this time. Strange that he made each turn on the route almost without thinking, as though it was still a natural place for him to be going. Just the same, Max couldn't get over the fact that the woman Frank had partnered him with was her.

Max tried to quit seeing all the emotions that had flashed across her face last night, but she'd always been lousy at hiding them. His stomach clenched slightly as he recalled the hurt look she'd worn when he'd refused to let her give her version of the Carpenter case.

But there was a reason for that, and the reason was that it didn't matter. No matter what she said, her actions during the Carpenter case remained a breach of ethics. Nothing she said would ever be enough to make up for her costing him his position at the company he'd worked his entire adult life to be an important part of.

Knowing that no answer would ever satisfy him was one of the things that had made it easier for him to go to Vegas. And besides, Kimberly had walked away. She'd gotten up and walked out of Kessler's office without looking back. It had seemed as if things were finished. As if they had to be.

He didn't like it—not professionally, not personally.

But it had seemed as if the smart thing to do was to move on with his life and what had been left of his career. And the smart thing to do now was not to think about the past, as he'd told her last night. Looking back wouldn't do either of them any good.

Max parked his car outside her building and stepped out into one of the first truly hot days of summer. The sun beat down from a cloudless sky, the only reprieve a gentle breeze that whispered through the trees lining the midcity sidewalk. Max liked days like this—hot and bright—better than the softer days of a California spring or fall. He liked extremes, always had. That's why he'd ended up being a P.I.

Well, the next few days, he thought as he strolled into the lobby, should definitely be extreme enough for him. And admittedly, he'd feel better if he were working with anyone else besides Kimberly Brandt, but he knew he couldn't keep dwelling on that. He had to get on with the business of catching Carlo Coletti.

When he knocked, she came to the door in faded jeans and a T-shirt. He knew it was ludicrous, but for some reason he'd been expecting to see her in that blue dress again. Her shoulder-length hair, which had been elegantly curled and styled last night, now fell around her face in a way that struck him as windblown, and her blue jeans looked soft and comfortable above sock-covered feet. He missed the obvious attributes of the dress immediately—she looked much plainer than she had last night—yet a rivulet of warmth trickled through him when he least expected it. Maybe her casual look reminded him of lazy afternoons spent driving nowhere with the top down, or of rainy days spent on the couch watching old movies and eating pizza between kisses.

Jeez, shake it off, Tate. He'd gotten lost there for a minute, but he was back now. He forced himself to meet her eyes, although just as quickly, she lowered her gaze to her own T-shirt. "What are you staring at?"

Damn. He'd been looking her up and down as though she wore a negligee instead of a loose T-shirt and jeans. He gave his head a light shake. "Nothing."

"Look," she said belligerently, "if I was supposed to be dressed in character already, you should have mentioned it."

He pushed past her into the apartment, not inclined to explain himself. "What you're wearing is fine for now. Where's your stuff?" He looked around the room at the familiar clutter and the antique furniture she liked, and spotted it himself—a garment bag tossed across the couch and a tapestry suitcase on the floor.

"It's right there—"

But he had already picked both of them up and was headed for the door. "Come on, let's get moving."

"If we're in a race, Tate, I should probably at least put on some shoes, don't you think?"

He stopped and looked back at her from the hallway, unamused. When had she become such a comedian? "Hurry up," he told her.

The way he saw it, he didn't have time to wait on her, and he didn't have time to think about past days spent with her, either. There was a job to be done and the sooner it was done the better. Then he could get on with his life.

MAX'S PORSCHE HUGGED the curves of the road that led from Kimberly's apartment toward Beverly Hills. Out of the corner of her eye, Kimberly watched him drive. His strong hands gripped the wheel tightly, but he leaned his long, sturdy body back in the seat like a man completely comfortable with himself. That was Max, she thought. He'd never lacked confidence.

"Nice day, huh?" she asked.

"Yeah." Short and clipped.

Yep, he had plenty of confidence, but manners had never been his strong suit.

She tried again a few minutes later, asking how his parents were doing. "Fine," he replied, eyes glued on the road.

All right, she got the hint. He wasn't disposed to making small talk.

And it was probably just as well. After all, they weren't buddies. They weren't pals. They were two people doing a job together. That was all.

"You should put your seat belt on," she told him anyway. She'd always been big on seat belts and always noticed when people weren't wearing them.

But he simply cast her an annoyed look in reply.

"The way you drive, you'll need it. Put it on."

After an irritated sigh, Max reached over his shoulder for the belt, muttering something below his breath.

"What?" Kimberly snapped. "I couldn't quite hear you."

"I was just saying," he enunciated insultingly, "that I forgot what a seat belt fanatic you are."

Kimberly rolled her eyes and crossed her arms, then turned to peer out the window.

"We should probably talk about our covers," he said

then, surprising her with even that bit of conversation and the almost cordial tone, too.

She nodded. "All right."

He gave her a short glance, then looked back to the road. "We'll keep our first names and my last one, making you Kimberly Tate."

Kimberly nodded again, wishing she didn't like the sound of that so much. This was not a good way to start her freshly reactivated plan of not thinking about him like that.

"I'm a stockbroker. I work for Finch and Company downtown, and I bring home half a mil every year. I've been with the company for ten years and was made a partner after five. I'm a Los Angeles native and so are you. We met in college at UCLA. As for our families, should it come up, we'll keep them as they are—same names, same backgrounds, same everything. It'll be a lot less for us to remember."

"What about me?" she asked.

"What *about* you?"

"What do *I* do?"

"You sit at home all day and be rich. You bask in luxury."

What a drag, Kimberly thought. Then an idea hit her. "Maybe I'm bored with you."

He turned to glare at her.

"Tate, the road!" she snapped.

He turned his eyes back to driving and Kimberly said, "See what I mean about the seat belt?" He ignored her, so she went on. "Anyway, I was thinking about why I would be interested in sleeping with this guy. So maybe it's because I'm bored. Bored with my life of luxury. Bored with you."

"Not possible."

His voice came without inflection as it had last night when he'd told her how hot she was. And she thought of arguing that it certainly *was* possible in the given scenario, but then she remembered the way Max made love. Polite he wasn't, but generous in bed—yes. He put his whole self, his whole soul, into the act. And she didn't know if he was thinking about the same thing, too—the way they used to make love for hours at a time until they were both exhausted and completely sated, but all things considered, she decided it would be simpler not to argue. "Okay then, if that's not the problem, why *would* I consider sleeping with this guy?"

"Maybe you're getting back at me."

"What did you do?"

"Cheated on you."

"You wouldn't," she said, fearful that it sounded more like a jealous plea than a statement. Asinine thoughts of the mysterious Julie came to mind.

"Why not?"

She took a deep breath and felt something slightly wicked, and slightly seductive, shroud her attitude. "Wait until you see me in the dress I'm wearing to dinner tonight, Tate," she told him. "Trust me. You wouldn't."

"OH MY GOD."

Max's car had just emerged from a grove of billowing storybook trees on the winding driveway that led to their borrowed mansion. The home before them boasted two incredibly tall columns that stretched from the expansive front porch to an arch at the top of the third story. Part brick, part white stucco, it reminded Kimberly of homes she'd seen on *Lifestyles of the Rich and Famous*. Nestled deep in the wooded hills, it made her think of a fairy-tale paradise.

"Get used to it," Max told her as she continued to gape. The car came to a halt in the circular driveway that fronted the mansion and Kimberly stumbled out of it, her eyes still exploring the splendor of it all. "You live here, you know. You can't seem too amazed by anything."

"I've got all day to work on that," she told him. "But for now, I can't help it—I'm pretty amazed."

"There's a pool. Did you bring a suit?"

Kimberly glanced over her shoulder at him and nodded, then returned her gaze to the house. She'd figured no decent mansion would be caught dead without a pool. Now that she saw the place, she was surprised it didn't have two or three.

"What's it like?"

She turned to give him her full attention. "What's what like?"

"Your swimsuit."

Despite the suggestion in the question, Kimberly knew it had nothing to do with *him*. It had to do with their job. "Yes, it's a two-piece. Our guest should love it."

He nodded at her, then quickly shifted his focus to getting her stuff from the car, but not before she thought she detected an unexpected glimmer of personal interest twinkling in his eyes. So maybe it *wasn't* just a business question. Her stomach raced with the idea that he might still be attracted to her....

But damn it! She stomped her foot on the ground to

punctuate her annoyance with herself. *Why did she even care? She was here to arouse the bad guy, not Max.*

Still, she couldn't help it if Max was aroused, too, could she? After all, she was only doing her job. Arousal didn't necessarily mean romance—often the two weren't even connected—but how could she help letting her mind wander in that direction? Her heart resumed its racing, but she tried to keep it under control as much as possible.

"Something wrong?"

She looked up with innocent eyes as Max rounded the car with her bags. "No. Why?"

"I thought you were stepping on a bug or something." He looked toward the foot she'd just stomped.

But Max wasn't the only one who could avoid unwanted conversations, she decided. "Let's go inside. I want to look around." And she rushed ahead toward the door.

BEYOND THE FOYER, which was lined with Mexican tile, the immense house stretched in all directions. A bright, spacious family room with a vaulted ceiling and huge picture windows that looked out on the pool area caught Kimberly's eye. To the right was a crisp white kitchen with a cooking island and a breakfast nook with another picture window.

In complete awe, Kimberly wandered the length of the nearest hallway, finding an elegant dining room filled with massive oak furniture. Renaissance art graced the walls. She next discovered an office and a library, a billiards room and a plush bathroom big enough to house a small family. She stumbled through a door into the three-car garage to find one spot empty;

however, a gray Mercedes and a jade-green Jaguar convertible sat neatly where they belonged.

Returning to the foyer on the route she'd traveled, she found Max wearing an annoyed look as he waited for her at the bottom of the curving staircase she'd glimpsed when she'd come inside. "Do you mind?" he muttered. "This thing weighs a ton." He motioned to the suitcase clutched in his right fist.

Kimberly merrily took the garment bag from his other hand. "Shoes," she explained of the suitcase. "Lots of them." Then she went past him on the stairs, still in wonder over the spectacular home she would call her own for the next few days. She didn't normally go for the contemporary look, but this house combined modern things with touches of old elegance in a way that filled her senses.

Once upstairs, she dragged her garment bag on another quick exploratory excursion, this time finding bedroom after bedroom, each decorated with its own specific theme and style. None of the lavish rooms appeared lived in, so Kimberly suspected they were all guest rooms.

Searching for the master bedroom, she glanced over her shoulder to find Max, still looking irritated at her amazement. But she didn't care. This place was *too* fabulous, and she thought that if he was smart, he'd let her get the wonderment out of her system before their guest arrived later.

In the meantime, she was ready to unload the garment bag. "Um, where is our—"

"That way." He pointed to the end of the hall she hadn't yet approached, and she headed in that direction, instantly glad he hadn't let her finish the sentence.

She was overwhelmed enough at the moment without being forced to start thinking about their sleeping arrangements.

She burst through the double doors that led to the master suite and released a heartfelt gasp, completely thunderstruck by what lay before her. Four tall, polished cherry posts emerged from the enormous bed. Wrought-iron bars connected the posts at the top from which a wide swath of filmy white fabric cascaded like a chiffon waterfall. Beneath the canopy, the lavishly dressed bed was adorned with more throw pillows than Kimberly had ever seen in one place. The bedroom's cathedral ceiling featured skylights, and a small fireplace graced one corner of the room, where two stylish easy chairs sat on either side of a low marble table.

Kimberly flung her garment bag on the bed and spun to face Max, who lingered in the doorway. "Have you seen this? It's gorgeous!"

But it would seem that Max never smiled anymore. "That it is," he agreed dryly, stepping into the room and lowering her suitcase to the floor. "You'll also find a huge master bath with a tub set in marble and a walk-in closet big enough to be a bedroom. But, Brandt, *you own all this stuff*. So it's no big deal, remember? Get used to it."

She hated his tone. Did he have to take all the fun out of *everything*? "Relax," she snipped at him. "I *will* get used to it. And I'll know every inch of it by heart before tonight. But for now, is it so horrible for you to let me enjoy it for a minute?"

"I'm not paying you to enjoy anything. I'm paying

you to do what you're supposed to do. Think you can handle that?"

She turned to look at him. He'd just succeeded in draining every bit of youthful joy from her heart. She didn't say anything—she didn't have to. His little innuendo was completely clear. "Then I guess we'd better get to work," she finally said, using her most mocking tone.

But when would she learn? A little mocking never daunted Max. "Yes. We'd better."

Max then showed Kimberly the dresser drawers and closet space that had been cleared for her. The idea of putting her things in places that really belonged to other people seemed a little creepy, but she took it in stride. And she tried to hide her astonishment at the size of the closet, too, lest Max think she was having too good a time on the job.

"Most importantly," Max told her as he crossed the room, "is this." He lifted a painting from the wall and revealed a safe. "The combination is simple. Thirty, thirty-one, thirty-two." Even more simple to remember, Kimberly thought, since she'd just turned thirty.

She watched as Max turned the knob on the lock three times, then opened the safe door and pulled out a round black velvet box that measured at least a foot in diameter. He thrust it into her hands and she reached down to lift the lid.

"What's in— Oh!" Inside, diamonds and a few emeralds and sapphires sparkled against the dark velvet. Kimberly gaped at the jewels, then raked her hand through them to scoop up necklaces and bracelets that dripped like streams of shimmering water through her fingers.

"Fake, of course," Max pointed out.

She'd figured that, but they were still beautiful. "What if our guy's a jewelry expert?"

"Good question," he said, and the way things were going, she was surprised he'd conceded something even as small as that. "They're not *cheap* fakes. They're as good as fake gets, supplied by my client. Unless Carlo has a jeweler's loupe in his pocket, he won't be able to tell. Besides, his thefts are sudden and quick— he doesn't have time to analyze the goods. So we should be fine on that count."

Kimberly closed the box and handed it back to Max, who returned it to the safe and locked the door. "Practice opening the safe later," he told her, "and familiarize yourself with the jewelry so you'll know how all the clasps work and that sort of thing."

She nodded, then turned toward the garment bags that lay on the bed. The bed that they would supposedly...*share?*

She guessed it was time to bite the bullet, act professional, and ask him just what his plans were for that. "Where...um, will everyone sleep?" She posed the question casually with her back to him.

"Everyone?"

"Well, you and me. And Carlo," she added, turning to face him. "And while we're on the subject, just why does he think you've invited him here?"

"Stocks," Max answered confidently. "Carlo wants to learn about the stock market and I'm just the guy to teach him."

"You are?"

"I know enough to fake it. When he expressed an interest, I suggested we get together one evening. I'd been hanging out with him for a few nights by then, so it didn't seem odd to invite him to dinner."

"And why does he think he's spending the night?"

"He doesn't necessarily, yet. But according to all the victims I've talked with, he gets chummy fast and then finds a way to prod the invitation."

Kimberly nodded, then realized she'd never let Max answer her original question. Her chest tightened as she brought it back up. "So, about the sleeping arrangements..."

"Carlo will sleep in one of the guest rooms," Max said. "You and I, of course, will sleep in here."

She looked back and forth between him and the bed, half surprised at his answer, and half surprised that she actually thought it sounded like such an awful idea. After all, despite the front she was putting up, in her heart of hearts, she'd almost already admitted to herself that the idea of sleeping next to Max turned her insides to jelly, no matter how much he disliked her. Now, however, faced with doing just that, her muscles tensed and her stomach churned. And if being with Max was something she really wanted, would it make her feel sick like this? So maybe she really *was* capable of not thinking of him like that. But she could ponder that later. Right now she had to deal with the matter at hand. "Do you think that's...appropriate?"

"Not particularly," he said. "But husbands and wives generally sleep together. Sleeping apart wouldn't do much to uphold our cover."

"Well, maybe we could just *pretend* to sleep together, but then later you could sneak out and use one of the guest rooms." She thought it was a pretty good suggestion.

Max shook his head. "He might get up in the night and realize we weren't together. It would look too suspicious. What if he were to look into the room while we're sleeping or something?"

Kimberly grimaced. "You think that's possible?"

"How would I know? The guy's a creep. Anything's possible. Which reminds me, we need to talk about actually nailing this jerk."

Well, Kimberly thought with a sigh, it would seem they'd settled that situation—sort of—so on to the next item of business. She lowered herself onto the ornate bed. "I'm listening."

"The only thing Carlo's seductions have in common is that he moves in for the kill when the husband's not home, and he ends up getting out of the house with jewelry, usually without the woman's knowledge at first. In one case, the woman went to take a shower after they'd slept together—taking off her jewelry beforehand—and when she came back, he was gone, along with the gems. Like I told you before, he actually took the jewelry off *my* client while she was sleeping. Another woman chose to refuse his advances, which is what will happen with you. She ran out of the room, at which point Carlo must have wiped her dresser clean of all the jewels, except what she was wearing."

"So I'll refuse his advances. But where will *you* be?"

"This is going to be a carefully orchestrated operation, Brandt. When the time comes to reel him in, I'll pretend to leave—to go to the office for some emergency or something—but I won't really leave. I'll actually be in the closet," he said, motioning to it. "Then you'll invite him into the bedroom to see the view from the balcony."

At this, Kimberly rose from the bed and padded over to check out the view. She hadn't realized it, but the balcony overlooked the pool and beyond that, a vast treed valley that stretched for miles, dotted with only two or three other mansions.

"I'll be videotaping the theft," Max continued, "and I'll also be there just in case you have any trouble fending the guy off. Hopefully, he'll take no for an answer, but use the opportunity to swipe the jewelry anyway."

Kimberly nodded. Sounded pretty simple.

"Any questions, Brandt?"

"None."

"All right then. I'll give you a few minutes to unpack your stuff." With that, he was out the door and Kimberly was alone in this fabulous room where a crime would soon take place. And where she and Max would soon share a bed. The thought bothered her more and more, actually making her stomach clench in pain. She didn't want to sleep next to Max tonight. Or any other night. There were simply too many old emotions involved. Old emotions that no longer mattered.

But Max had made it pretty clear that the point wasn't up for discussion. So Kimberly sighed and tried to move past it for the moment and onto more productive things.

Unpacking didn't take long. She added her array of dresses to the already filled closet, put her toothbrush and electric rollers in the bathroom, and stuck her bikini and lacy undies in the drawers provided. She had no intention of letting Carlo Coletti ever see her in anything lacy, of course, but it had seemed like a good thing to have around just in case he did something gross like go through her drawers. Besides, the character of Mrs. Max Tate, whom she would become this evening, didn't wear cotton panties like the ones Kimberly often did. Only the most luxurious of lace for Kimberly Tate, stockbroker's wife and femme fatale.

Max had explained to her already that the rest of the house was completely furnished and stocked with everything they needed for their stay. Before the day was through, she'd have to tour it carefully and find out the little things—where they kept the bath towels, what kind of food was on hand, how the alarm system worked. She'd have to make sure it seemed as if she and Max really lived there.

Of course, that was only part of it. They had to convince Carlo Coletti that they were married. Had Max really thought about that? She wandered back to the bed and let herself plop down on it to stare up at the vaulted ceiling. Perhaps she should address the question with him, but it was obviously a touchy subject. She didn't want to imply that they should or shouldn't do any specific married-seeming things in front of Carlo Coletti. Physical things, for instance. Still, she figured they'd have to. The thought made her shiver, just as when she imagined sharing this bed with him. Oh well, she guessed she had no choice but to cross that bridge when she came to it.

And maybe Max *did* have a plan. Maybe he was going to be one of those unaffectionate types of husbands, the ones who took their wives for granted and never paid them any attention. As cold as Max was acting to her, it would be an easy role for him to take on.

He seemed to think he was the only one who had suffered any losses because of the Carpenter case. He blamed her for everything, though, so of course he wouldn't be sitting around thinking about how *her* life had been affected. She'd lost her job, which she'd loved, and she'd lost him, whom she'd also loved, all in one fell swoop. Not to mention that at the time she'd also been dealing with the very fresh news that her mother had cancer.

Two months of depression later, Kimberly had pulled herself together enough to take a job with another company. Unfortunately, the guy she'd worked for wasn't as good as Max, and business was bad. When the agency finally folded just over a year ago, she'd signed on with Frank.

She'd recovered from the blows she'd taken during that period, but she considered it the blackest spot of her entire past, for reasons both professional and personal.

Oh sure, she'd made mistakes under Max's tutelage, but she'd never completely screwed up a case. And she'd never been fired from a job before in her life.

Max's way of handling what had happened had shown her that he obviously hadn't cared for her very much. Sure, she'd been the one to walk out of that office, but he hadn't stopped her. Then he'd gone to Las Vegas, just like that. Only then had she come to the conclusion that what they'd shared had been one-sided. Not sexually—she knew that—but in other ways. In emotional ways. She was glad she'd never said the words to him that had lingered in her heart whenever they were together—*I love you*. If any shred of doubt about how Max had felt had been left lingering in the back of her mind, seeing him again had killed it off entirely. It was clear that she'd been nothing to him.

But that's okay, she affirmed as a familiar hurt melted through her. *That's okay because you don't even want to share a bed with him. You don't want to be close to him.* The fact was, Kimberly was over Max. Completely and for good. As of right now, *he* was nothing to *her*, either.

MAX LAY on the plush leather couch in the big family room watching TV, trying to take it easy in the last few hours before the show began, and also trying to feel as if this place, this life, were *his*. Meanwhile, his pretend wife was in the kitchen digging through drawers and cabinets, getting herself familiar with things.

He didn't know why he'd made that crack about her handling the job earlier. He'd told himself this morning that he had to quit that crap if they were going to work together with any success, but it had leaked out like air escaping a punctured balloon.

Three years hadn't healed his mistrust of her. This was going to be hard, perhaps the hardest case of his career. Now it was being made even harder, not only by his fears of her screwing up or letting him down, but also because he had to own up to the fact that he was still attracted to her, which he'd have to forget or ignore or something. It was like he'd told Frank last night. If he wanted sex, he could get it. He certainly wouldn't attempt to get that or anything else from the woman who had betrayed him.

"Oh my God, we have caviar!"

Her voice sounded from somewhere in the kitchen behind him and he worked to hold in even the hint of a smile, whether she could see him or not. He couldn't start going soft on her. But that's what he remembered about Kimberly. How fascinated she could be by the world. How in awe.

Maybe that's why he'd given her such a hard time over her wonder regarding the house—he hadn't wanted to be reminded of her, of them together. And maybe that's why this morning he'd thought of those simple, easy times with her, those T-shirt-and-jeans times. He knew they'd done other things, too—gone out to dinner, gone to plays, to nightclubs—but she could find unmitigated joy just in eating ice cream or watching the rain fall. She wasn't like that all the time, though. When she was working, she was strictly business. But when work was done, she took the joys of life pretty seriously, and he'd liked that.

Suddenly, she came rushing into the room in a flurry, cutting into his thoughts and stirring up a small breeze. "Tate, I just thought of something!"

"What's that?"

"Dinner! Am I supposed to be cooking? Because if I am, what am I making? And how am I making it?" She waved her arms around in total panic. "I mean, I cook—you know I cook—but I don't...*cook*. Not like anything fancy. So...?"

He hesitated, feeling devilish for no reason and having no luck in pushing it down. "I thought maybe you'd learned, taken lessons or something," he said, trying to keep a straight face.

She widened her eyes in what was obviously sheer horror. "Why on earth would you think that?"

"Well, we haven't seen each other in a while. I thought maybe you'd taken up a hobby."

He thought it obvious that he was only kidding, but she looked even more distressed. And he guessed he could understand it easily enough. This was the first time he'd done anything even remotely lighthearted since laying eyes on her yesterday.

And actually, kidding her was a bad idea. Hadn't he just told himself not to go soft on her? There would be enough of that once they assumed their roles as husband and wife.

"Tate, if you were going to write things like that into my character, you could've at least told me and I'd have studied a cookbook last night or something. Now, what are we going to do about dinner?"

This time he made sure to keep his face expressionless. It was much safer not to let her know he was even mildly entertained by anything she did. "Don't worry. I have a chef coming at five-thirty to start dinner. She'll serve us at seven, then clean up the mess when we're through."

Kimberly let out a sigh of relief. "A chef. That's good. Thanks for letting me suffer through that, by the way."

He got the idea she might be waiting for a comeback from him, some teasing remark, but he didn't oblige.

Then she was suddenly looking around, no longer in awe, but as if something terrible had just struck her. "You know, Tate, this is a big place. Shouldn't we have housekeepers or something? Shouldn't we have a *full-time* chef?"

"Already thought of that," he said, remaining emotionless. He'd contemplated hiring people to fill those roles, but he hadn't particularly wanted anyone extra around, considering that Carlo might be dangerous and anything could happen. "I'll just mention to Carlo that our housekeeper, who also happens to be our chef, asked for the weekend off," he explained. "So when she leaves, it won't seem weird."

"Ah," Kimberly said, nodding. "Okay. That's good. That will work."

"Of course it will," he answered absently. From his peripheral vision, he saw her staring at him while he watched TV, since he'd made a point of returning his attention to it already. Maybe she was waiting for him to say something else, keep this merry little conversation going, but it wasn't going to happen.

This was simple if he could only remember the rules.

No more Mr. Nice Guy.

SCENTS OF SOMETHING succulent met Kimberly's nose as she moved delicately down the stairway in three-inch heels. But she couldn't look forward to dinner, or enjoy her surroundings, or even anticipate the thrill of satisfaction in the job that was about to begin. Her chest felt tight and her throat did, too. The butterflies that had invaded her stomach while she dressed had suddenly begun releasing hand grenades in there now. She wasn't nervous about the job. She wasn't nervous about Carlo Coletti. She was nervous about Max. About Max seeing her.

Odd, for a second there when they'd been discussing the whole dinner thing, she'd thought she'd sensed something new in him, something fresh and almost friendly. A hint of a smile and maybe even a soft tone. But things had changed quickly as he'd put up his typical wall between them and she'd been forced to change her opinion. Max, friendly? Nope, she'd clearly been imagining things. Now she had to wonder all the more how things would be between them as they progressed into the charade, and as she became his "wife," the femme fatale.

At the bottom of the stairs she approached a gilt-framed mirror that captured her image from head to toe. Her hair was bunched up on top of her head, tiny wisps of it falling over her cheeks and nape. Along with a "wedding ring" pilfered from the black box upstairs, she wore a pair of fake diamond earrings that dangled and sometimes tickled her neck, and a thin diamond necklace that she thought would be a teaser for their guest. But the real event was clearly taking place *below* her neck.

The dress was slinky, black and short, and hugged her every curve. Tiny straps held up the low-cut bodice, which was built for cleavage and definitely delivered. She was pretty sure she'd been a size smaller when she'd bought this dress and it had looked fine on her then, hanging looser and more comfortably. But now...well, she finally understood how it was *meant* to fit. She barely recognized herself, and she couldn't help wondering how Max would react.

She tried to tell herself that her nervousness was because she wanted to please him as an employee wishes to please a boss, that she wanted him to think she was the perfect woman for this job. But it was more than that. Ever since she'd started feeling this way, she'd tried to tell herself that it *wasn't* more than that, but it was. And what was worse, it was something *sexual*. Since the moment she'd put on this dress and thought of Max seeing her in it, her entire body had been charged with an undeniable sexual tension.

And here she'd thought she was over him. Completely and totally.

"How do you explain *that?*" she whispered, scowling at her reflection in the mirror.

Perhaps it had to do with the nature of this case, she decided. It centered on sex, after all. Unfortunately, the guy who would want her was going to be an icky, lecherous thief. But the guy who was supposed to be her husband—her protector, sort of—was *not* icky. Far from it. So that was it. She was being forced to think about sex because of the case and the way it had caused her to dress and she had to vent those sexual feelings in *some* direction. That meant Max.

She smiled into the mirror, feeling much better. She still didn't like the way she felt, but she'd decided it made sense and that she'd given herself a logical explanation. Her desire for Max would go away, she promised herself. It was just a preliminary feeling brought on by the role she was being asked to play.

Hearing footsteps in the hallway, she turned to see Max enter the large foyer where she stood. He gave her a long, slow perusal that made her feel hot inside. And that also made her realize everything she'd just told herself was obviously a crock.

"Well?" she finally said.

"Sexy as sin itself," he replied, his voice low.

She swallowed hard because she thought she'd detected just a trace of emotion this time, just a faint hint of passion. Enough to send a wave of heat traveling the length of her spine.

Oh yes, that crap about feeling sexual because it was part of the job was a crock. No truth in it whatsoever. She wanted the guy. God help her, but she did. As for thinking she was over him because she didn't want to sleep next to him? More bull. Because right now, right at this moment, she *did* want to sleep next to him. Only she didn't want to sleep. She wanted to do other things, and lots of them. And it was hitting her hard, nearly taking her breath away. If she'd been sick before...well, she was sick now, too. Sick with wanting it, over feeling so much for him, even when he obviously hated her. But this time the sickness didn't diminish her desire. Nope, not one little bit.

Nonetheless, she had to pull herself together and try to continue the conversation. "So you think he'll like me then?"

He flashed her a knowing look that seemed to say, "Quit playing games." Then he raked his eyes over her once more, fueling the fire inside her. "Yeah. He'll like you."

Wearing a black Armani suit, Max looked pretty good himself. Okay, more than pretty good. Really, really good. Which was part of why she was becoming so painfully aware of how much she wanted him. "Aren't you overdressed?" she asked for the sake of curiosity.

He shook his head. "I just got home from work. I'm a stockbroker, remember."

"Oh, right." And she hadn't meant to imply that she minded at all. In fact, she couldn't help thinking that they probably made a very striking couple.

It was only a shame that it was all pretend.

She suddenly felt nervous and decided she'd better be prepared for whatever was coming because, knowing Max, she wouldn't have much of a choice either way. So she took a deep breath and said, "Max, have you thought about...how to convince this guy we're married?"

He didn't answer, and she felt stupid now, so she went on. "I mean, we don't *act* married."

"We're not *acting* married because the guy's not *here* yet," he said, looking suddenly and unduly worried. "When he *gets* here, *then* we'll act married. Frank said you could pull this off. You're not going to let me down again, are you?"

The words hit her like a blow to the gut. She couldn't believe his contempt! His veiled, snide comments were one thing, but this was, this was... Oh, she was so furious she could barely think straight! As for wanting him...well, he'd very efficiently squelched all the passion that had been flooding her, which was just fine with her. She instantly resolved that she wouldn't sleep with him if he were the last man on earth, and she thought of telling him that, but decided it would be more appropriate to the conversation to say instead, "Of course I can pull it off, you arrogant jerk! And no, I'm not going to let you down. In fact, I'm going to prove to you once and for all just how good a P.I. I am."

"Well, that would be a pleasant surprise."

She sneered at him, for lack of any better response, because the only one she could think of was the I-wouldn't - sleep - with - you - if - you - were - the - last - man-on-earth thing, which might tip him off she was thinking about sex, and she wasn't about to give him the pleasure of knowing that.

Then she made a concerted effort to calm down, because Carlo Coletti would be here any minute and she couldn't let Max rile her like this—she had to stay professional. She drew in a deep, cleansing breath, tried to banish all the crazy, mixed-up emotions from her mind, then spoke in a very calm tone. "I only wanted to know if you'd given any thought to how—"

The chime of the doorbell cut her off. "Show time," Max said.

What timing! She rolled her eyes. Max placed both his strong hands on her shoulders. "Are you ready?"

Not particularly, but she didn't exactly have a choice, did she? She was completely determined to show Max that she could do her job, so she nodded. "Yes. I'm ready."

"Then here we go," he said. And he opened the door.

"Max!" said the man standing on the other side, who was surprisingly youngish and tall and blond, and even kind of handsome. Still, just viewing him from where she stood behind Max, Kimberly could sense the smarmy guy lurking beneath the nice sports jacket—it was something tailored clothes and a handsome face couldn't hide.

"Carlo, come in."

Max stepped back and motioned Carlo inside, and then Carlo's eyes fell on Kimberly and he stopped cold. Yep, he was sleazy all right. He looked at her in *that* way, the way men couldn't see, but women could sense, the way that felt dirty and ugly and bad. You'd have to be in a desperate place, Kimberly thought instantly, to let this guy get the best of you, but that wasn't her concern right now.

"My God, Max!" he said, still looking at Kimberly. She smiled her way through it, even forcing herself to meet his gaze. He looked like a guy who'd just won the jackpot at Caesar's Palace. "*This* is a beautiful woman, Max!"

"Honey, meet Carlo Coletti," Max said with a huge smile.

She held out her hand and Carlo took it, holding on to it too long, while he extended his other hand to squeeze her elbow—always the giveaway of a true lech. "It's a great pleasure to meet such a lovely lady."

Kimberly cringed inwardly. "It's very nice to meet you, too, Carlo," she returned, sounding incredibly pleasant, even to her own ears.

Max stepped forward and slid his arm around her, resting his hand firmly on her bare shoulder. "And Carlo, this is my treasure of a wife, Kimberly."

And then Max kissed her.

3

HE KISSED HER long and slow and deep. His tongue glided past her lips, draining the breath from her, leaving her completely weak. Kimberly had no choice but to throw her arms around his neck and hold on or else she'd faint with the utter deliciousness of him.

Well, this answered one question. Apparently he'd given this charade some thought.

Actually, his kiss answered several questions, the rest of which had to do with her wanting him with every ounce of her being, despite his holding her responsible for lots of bad things in his life. She definitely did. And it was definitely way out of her control.

His tongue touching hers was like electricity and it shot a bolt of lightning straight to the lace panties she wore. His mouth had an unusual way of feeling both soft and hard at the same time—something she remembered and cherished. She clutched at him still, the hair at the nape of his neck held tenderly in her fist, her entire body pulsing with the power of his incredible kiss.

And then he was gone, pulling back, ending it. Kimberly tried to breathe again and get her balance, all the while hoping she looked sexy and sophisticated in spite of the fact that Max had just kissed her senseless.

"You'll have to forgive me, Carlo," Max said, tinting

his voice with masculine laughter. "I don't mean to be so rude. But I was...overcome. When you have a woman like this, you spend every second wanting to be alone with her."

Kimberly still couldn't quite believe he'd done it. It seemed like an impossible thing to have happened...and not a smart thing to do, characterwise. Now, if he'd been playing Rocko the strip-club owner and she'd been Bimbo the stripper, maybe. But he was a stockbroker. They were supposed to be dignified people. She looked up at Carlo for a reaction.

"Oh, don't apologize," he said. "I understand perfectly." He took the opportunity to cast her a wildly lustful look that made her want to retch, but instead she smiled and hoped it came through in her eyes as the truth. She grasped the idea instantly then—Carlo was as sleazy as sleazy got, and Max had played him correctly. Carlo didn't realize classy people didn't make out while greeting guests at the door. He only wished it could have been him. It had done nothing but fuel his desire for her.

"Shall we go have a drink before dinner?" Max suggested, and she flashed him a smile, too, because that suddenly seemed to be her job in the last two minutes—kissing and flashing smiles. In return, he smiled back, this really great smile that pretty much melted everything inside her to molten lava all over again. To top it off, he even put his hand at the small of her back to escort her down the hall.

As they walked toward the living room, and Max and Carlo made manly small talk about Max's Porsche, the past few minutes hit Kimberly anew. *Max had kissed her!* Full, sensuous and passionate! The kind of kiss that young girls dreamed of and the kind of kiss that older girls wanted more and more of. Oh, how she wanted more! She'd wanted more the moment his mouth had left hers. It had been a kiss that drenched your soul in desire and heat and left you knowing that the world would never quite be the same again.

She released a long, deep sigh and let the afterglow of it roll through her. And then she remembered.

Oh God, she'd forgotten so quickly.

It was only pretend.

"TO NEW FRIENDS," Carlo said, clinking his glass against Kimberly's, then Max's.

"New friends," Max echoed.

Kimberly only smiled. Like before, it seemed adequate.

But now that she'd recovered—somewhat—from Max's unexpected kiss, she decided it was time to get to work. "So, Carlo, Max tells me you want to learn about the stock game." She took a step closer to him and gave her head what she hoped was a slightly flirtatious tilt.

Carlo smiled, almost sincerely, but he blew it when his gaze dropped ever so briefly to her breasts before rising back to her eyes. "Yes, it's something I've always been interested in, but never had the time to pursue."

"Then you're not in banking?" she asked, not only to draw out his cover, but also to make him think she was interested in finding out more about him.

Carlo shook his head. "Shipping."

"As in boats?" Kimberly asked, confused.

He shook his head again, a smile on his face. "My

company ships merchandise, mostly glassware and fragile items."

"Ah," she said, flicking a short glance to Max. She'd expected him to come up with something a little more exotic or at least impressive. "And how did you meet Max?"

"We both frequent Chester's," Max answered for him. Kimberly knew the upscale bar on the ground floor of one of the ritzy office buildings downtown.

"Max is quite a pool shark," Carlo said.

"That he is," she agreed, although she'd never seen Max play pool before. But he'd always told her that a good P.I. possessed a variety of skills that helped him fit into any social setting, and she supposed this was one example. A guy who could play a decent game of pool probably made friends in a bar much easier than a guy who didn't.

"Do *you* play?" Carlo asked her then, a suggestive light twinkling in his eyes.

She almost released a laugh at what she was sure he had intended as a double entendre, but instead held her response to a flirtatious grin. So far, that seemed to be the only skill required from her in this particular case, but when the time came to make their way to the dining room, Kimberly steeled herself, knowing things were bound to get a lot more challenging, starting now.

MAX LET CARLO TAKE the place at the head of the table, and he and Kimberly took the seats on either side. It was strategic placement—let Carlo feel important, get close to Kimberly. At the same time, though, he hoped Carlo wouldn't move in on her too quickly. The idea of the slimeball sliding his hand onto her knee beneath the table rankled him.

Max hated the way the guy looked at her. That was why he had kissed her like that when Carlo had walked in the door. It was as if he'd thought acting territorial would protect her. He knew he was *supposed* to want Carlo to react to her this way, but it had happened a little easier than he'd expected. Max now realized it was going to be a little tougher to play dumb than he had anticipated. His ego would definitely take a beating as he let Carlo steal his "wife" right from under his nose while he pretended to be oblivious. Especially when Carlo was such a piece of garbage.

Next to him, Carlo leered at Kimberly, which was, of course, just what he was supposed to do. But already, Max felt the need to interrupt. "So, Carlo, what do you think of the place?" He motioned to their surroundings like a man who was the king of his castle.

"Fabulous, Max. Incredible." He quickly turned his gaze back to Kimberly. "And a wife like this to share it all with? You've got the life, pal. What I wouldn't give to be in your shoes."

Subtle, the guy wasn't.

"Oh, now, Carlo," Kimberly answered in a half-bashful, half-flattered tone, "you're too kind." She even fluttered her eyelashes at him like a teenager in heat. Subtlety wasn't her strong suit, either, but, Max remembered, her job right now was not to be subtle—it was to be *available.* Another rankling idea.

"Where'd you find this beauty, Max, old buddy?"

Old buddy? I'll old buddy you, he thought, but he reined in his irritation. "We met in college."

Carlo's leer managed to increase and Max imagined

thoughts of naughty coeds dancing through Carlo's head. Kimberly was leering right back at him, her eyes wide, her lips pretty and pouty with lipstick the color of red wine.

"I knew the moment I saw her," Max said without planning it, "that she was the woman for me." He saw Kimberly turn her hazel eyes on him, which had been his hope, although he didn't know why. He remembered how some days her eyes seemed more brown, other days gold as amber, and how, at still other times, they would glitter green. Tonight they took on a warm honey-colored shade. He didn't hesitate to hold the gaze. "She was wearing a short red skirt and a white blouse and she had a great tan. It was October."

He watched her go still, then swallow hard, and he liked the effect the words had had on her. Because that really *was* what she'd been wearing on the day they'd met, although it hadn't been at college. It had been on an elevator at the Kessler Agency's building. She'd heard him tell someone he was a P.I. and she'd started asking him questions about it.

"We had lunch," she reminded him, her voice silky.

Yes, he recalled, her questions had turned into an invitation for lunch, and lunch had turned into a job for her.

"You ordered quiche," he said, their eyes still locked.

He could tell this one surprised her—she'd always accused him of having a bad memory for details. "That's right."

"What did *I* have?" he quizzed her.

Her expression turned slightly saucy with the game they were playing. "You think I don't remember?"

"Prove me wrong."

"An Italian sub," she replied smoothly. "Extra pepperoni."

He grinned slightly at the correct answer.

"So..." Carlo interrupted uncertainly, drawing Max back to the present. He knew the schmuck was desperate to be the center of attention again, which Max apparently needed reminding. What had he been doing strolling down memory lane like that, anyway? He couldn't explain it, except to again chalk it up to his ego, something he certainly hadn't expected to come into play here. He'd have to squelch it in the future.

"Sorry about that, Carlo." Ready to change the mood, Max said, "Excuse me for a moment," then rose from his chair and went to the doorway that connected with the kitchen. There he found Mrs. Leland, the woman he'd hired to cook for them this evening. "Could you bring the wine I have chilling, please?"

Returning to the table, he found his guest already ogling his "wife" again, something he'd have to start pretending he didn't see. But maybe, he told himself, his departure from "oblivious husband" had been good. If the jerk truly got a charge out of stealing the wife away from the adoring spouse, Max had set it up perfectly; it sure hadn't scared Carlo away.

Kimberly looked back and forth between the two men. She couldn't have been more weirded out. She had two guys vying for her attention—every woman's fantasy. Except that one of them was a sleazy toad and the other one was pretending. Swell. Okay, so it wasn't a *perfect* fantasy.

"Those are exquisite earrings," Carlo said. Then he actually reached out and diddled her earlobe with his fingertip. She wanted to convulse with disgust. "Lovely necklace, too," he purred. Soon his fingers were there, touching it, playing with it, and her entire body went tense, even as she told herself, *Smile, damn it. Smile at the jerk.*

"That's just a bauble," Max said across from her as Carlo continued to examine the necklace.

She turned her gaze on Max. Did he look as tense as she felt? Or was she just imagining that?

"She picked it up on our last trip to New York," Max continued with a grin. "If you want to see Kimberly's *real* jewelry, you'll have to sweet-talk her into showing it to you."

Carlo practically glowed with lust at Max's suggestion, but he finally pulled his fingers away from her neck, thank goodness. "I'd love to take a look at it sometime."

"Max has been *very* generous," Kimberly said, and she smiled across the table at him. She glanced up then to see Mrs. Leland enter with the wine and start pouring it into the fluted crystal glasses before them.

"Kimberly has a weakness for diamonds, don't you, babe?" Max asked.

Babe. He used to call her that. Not in the too-forward, insulting way, but in the casual, endearing, that's-how-close-we-are way.

She swallowed. "Yes," she managed to say. "I have a horrible weakness for diamonds."

"She wears them constantly," Max went on. Kimberly thought at this point he might be pouring it on a bit thick, but he seemed to know what he was doing where Carlo was concerned, so she just let him ramble, waiting to see where it would lead. "Tonight, for instance, a casual dinner with a new friend and out come the diamonds."

She saw an opportunity and flashed another of her come-hither smiles. "Well, I wanted to look nice for Carlo and make a good impression on him."

"Oh, you do, and you have," Carlo gushed.

But Max kept right on going. "She actually wears them out shopping sometimes."

"Only to the better stores, honey," she insisted.

"And once, *once*—" Max paused to give another of those masculine just-between-us-guys laughs "—I actually found her wearing them as she sat by the pool."

"The pool?"

Kimberly gave a ridiculous giggle, warming to her part now. "It wreaked havoc on my tan lines, but I do enjoy the feel of them next to my skin."

Carlo closed his eyes a moment and murmured something too low for her to understand—probably some observation about tan lines or skin. So she blinked and continued looking lively and vibrant. "I'm sorry, I missed that. What did you say, Carlo?"

Unfortunately, he got hold of himself. "Oh, nothing. Just saying that I didn't realize you guys had a pool."

She flashed him an incredulous look and even lifted splayed fingers to her chest. "I wouldn't own a house without one. In fact, I find it rather small and keep bugging Max to build me a bigger one." The pool, in fact, was enormous, but she made a pouty face at Max anyway.

"Nothing I love more than a swimming pool," Carlo said.

"Really?" Max replied matter-of-factly. "Well, you'll have to come over for a swim sometime."

"Soon, perhaps," Kimberly added in a lilting voice.

Carlo tilted his head and glanced coyly back and forth between them. "You know..." he began, but then he stopped and shook his head. "Never mind."

"What is it?" Kimberly asked.

Carlo lowered his chin sheepishly. "Oh, it's nothing."

"No, really, what were you going to say?"

"Well." He stopped and shook his head almost helplessly. "I was just thinking that my place is being painted this weekend..."

"Actually, I've never heard you say where you live, Carlo," Max said, more from curiosity about Carlo's reply, Kimberly suspected, than anything else.

"Oh, I've got a huge condo near the beach. It's...being remodeled. That's why it's being painted. I just picked out my colors."

"Sounds lovely," Kimberly said, "but what does that have to do with...whatever we were talking about?" She giggled at her own forgetfulness, figuring that playing dumb might add to her assets in his eyes.

Again, Carlo looked hesitant. "Well, I was just thinking, if you guys weren't busy, that it might be a great time for me to catch some rays by the pool, but... I wouldn't want to impose, so just forget I said anything."

"Why should we forget it?" Kimberly replied. "I think it's a wonderful idea. Max and I have no plans at all this weekend, do we, honey?"

"None at all." Max gave his head a short shake.

"In fact, there's no need for you to go home and sleep in those nasty fumes," Kimberly went on. "Why don't you just stay here tonight, and tomorrow we can all enjoy the pool together."

Carlo feigned shock at such a generous offer. "Are you sure? It wouldn't be an imposition?"

His question struck her as quite silly, since he'd practically invited himself, but Kimberly found it easier just to play along. "Tomorrow's Saturday," she replied. "And we have plenty of guest rooms. So, why not? You don't mind, do you, Max?"

She shifted her gaze back to him and he smiled. "Of course not. We'd love to have you."

And *I'd* love to have *you*, Kimberly thought, her mind yanked mercilessly from her work just by looking into Max's eyes.

"Well, thanks. That's great," Carlo was saying, but Kimberly barely even heard him. Instead, she found herself turning her come-hither smile on Max then, glad she could do it under the guise of her role, but inside still wishing that it wasn't all just pretend.

AFTER THE SALAD, Mrs. Leland served salmon, rice and fresh bread. Kimberly listened as Max took the opportunity to talk stocks and bonds with Carlo—another impressive skill he'd apparently picked up somewhere along the way. She bowed out of the conversation other than to add an occasional comment to help keep Carlo focused on her.

As the charade went on, Kimberly found herself wading through the mire of wanting Max more and more with each passing minute. Even when she worked to bait Carlo with her flirtations, she stayed painfully aware of Max's presence, and couldn't keep her thoughts from straying to past times—better times—shared with him.

"Kimberly?"

She jolted to attention. "Huh?" She looked up to see Max and Carlo both rising from their chairs.

"I said," Max told her very calmly, "let's retire to the living room for a while." He raised his eyebrows at her as if to say, *Pay attention!* and she thought, *Swell, great way to show him what a good P.I. I am.*

But all Kimberly's bad feelings were quelled when she took a seat on the big white sofa in front of the fireplace and Max sat down next to her, sliding his arm around her shoulder. Her heart fluttered and a few other choice body parts did, as well. This husband-and-wife thing definitely had its benefits, even if it *was* only make-believe.

Carlo settled in a roomy chair near them and started looking a little antsy, but Max acted as if he didn't notice and proceeded to talk some more about his imaginary career in investments.

"Which reminds me," Max finally said, "I've got a business call to make—need to touch base with a colleague in Japan. Will you excuse me for a few minutes?"

As quick as that, he was gone, up off the couch and out of the room. Disappointment ran rampant through Kimberly's limbs. A business call? Now? She knew this meant it was time to get down to some more of *her* business by flirting with Carlo *in private* and letting him think she might be interested in him in *that* way.

It took Carlo about half a second to make the first move. He rose from his chair and joined her on the couch. Too close for her liking, but part of the job, she reminded herself. She'd done this kind of work on occasion before, so it wasn't something she didn't know how to handle. But most of the suspects weren't as outright lecherous as this guy. And she'd never before done this kind of work when her mind and body were so desperately tied up with wanting another man.

"Hi," he said. His eyes practically twinkled with the new seclusion they shared.

She made herself smile back at him, look a bit coquettish. "Hi."

Carlo reached out and fingered the thin shoulder strap of her dress. "You're a beautiful woman, Kimberly."

This guy really had to work on his originality, she thought, but she forged ahead. "Why, Carlo, you're going to make Max jealous with all these compliments."

"They're all true," he said. "But Max doesn't matter."

Wow, he was quick. She put on her best innocent face. "Max doesn't matter?"

"I just mean...he's not here right now. It's just me and you."

She nodded, for lack of a better move.

He withdrew his fingers from beneath the strap of her dress and once again slid them to the thin diamond necklace she wore. "I'm still quite taken by this, Kimberly."

"Thank you, Carlo."

"Is all of your jewelry truly this exquisite?"

Okay, he was more than quick—he was a regular speed demon—but she took the opening. "As Max said at dinner, this is really just a smallish piece. My collection upstairs consists of much more elaborate jewels."

Carlo nodded, looking very attentive. "So you keep them on the premises. Is that safe?"

She wanted to laugh and wondered for the first time just how stupid these victimized couples had been. She could only guess that maybe they hadn't come across as totally inviting as she and Max. Or perhaps the wives were truly attracted to Carlo. Kimberly herself saw straight through him for the slime he was, but if you didn't, well, she could imagine the things he said and the way he touched so freely being intimidating.

"Well, they're in a safe in our bedroom so I hope they're secure enough," she said after a brief hesitation. "If I kept them in some silly safe-deposit box somewhere, it would be much harder to wear them, wouldn't it?"

She giggled and Carlo joined in her laughter, gently lowering a hand to her knee. She tensed at the touch, but didn't let it show. "Say," he began, "maybe while we're waiting for Max to finish with his call, you could show me some of your prized gems. Hearing you talk about them has intrigued me."

Nope, too soon. She and Max hadn't even begun to synchronize the theft yet, and anything could happen. She knew Max had suggested Carlo ask her to see the jewelry, but she also knew that had been bait not meant for tonight. "Oh, we've got plenty of time for that...now that you're staying," she told Carlo. When she sensed him getting ready to lean closer, she rose to her feet. "How about some brandy?"

"All right," he muttered, obviously annoyed with her sudden departure.

As she hurried to the bar across the room, he stood

up and followed her. Jeez, he was a complete sleaze-ball.

Kimberly had familiarized herself with the liquor cabinet, so she pulled out a decanter half filled with brandy, along with two snifters. She poured one and handed it to him, and then poured another for herself. After recapping the decanter, she picked up her snifter and turned to find Carlo standing far too close for comfort.

"Let's toast," he said. "To diamonds. And to you. Two of the world's natural beauties."

MAX LEANED BACK in the big, dark leather chair in the study. He propped his feet on the desk and looked around. Built-in mahogany bookcases, housing old volumes with rich leather spines that he could smell, surrounded him. To his left, a huge picture window looked out on the front lawn. To his right, a framed map of the world hung on the wall. *If you had all this*, he thought, studying the map, *why would you need look any further?*

Carlo's words came back to him. *And a wife like this to share it all with? You've got the life, pal.* Carlo had been right about that....

Wait a minute.

The last thing Max needed was a wife like Kimberly and he knew it. Sure, he didn't like seeing Carlo all over her, but that didn't mean he was ready to marry her. Or even engage in any relationship at all. There was one thing he didn't have with Kimberly that was a major relationship essential—trust.

He'd left her alone with Carlo strictly to give the guy the opportunity to start making his moves, start trying to lure her away from Max while he wasn't around to fawn over her. He kind of hated doing that, but he knew Kimberly could handle it. She'd been a quick study at the P.I. thing until she loused up the Carpenter case. And that wasn't a skills problem—it was ethics.

Skills, she had, which was good, because she'd need them to handle this creep. And Frank wouldn't have sent her if he'd had any doubts that she could do it. Max had to admit, she had become a good actress since he'd last seen her. Maybe a little *too* good. She'd been fine with being bait before, but he'd never cast her as anything like this—a sexy, ready kind of woman. She was pulling it off without a hitch. It irritated Max to know Carlo thought she really liked him.

What a guy, this Carlo. Frankly, he was worse than Max had expected. He kind of wanted to kill the jerk, thinking about how excited the guy had gotten watching Max kiss her, hoping to steal her at the same time. Oh well, at least they'd wasted not even a minute making sure Carlo viewed Kimberly in a sexual light. Not that Max liked him thinking of her that way.

Just why the hell was that again? His ego, he reminded himself. Just his ego.

"Mr. Tate?"

Max looked up from his thoughts to see Mrs. Leland leaning through the office doorway. He was glad for the distraction—he was starting to obsess over this situation and he didn't like it. "Yes, Mrs. Leland?"

"I've finished cleaning up dinner, so I'll be going now."

"All right. Thank you for letting me know."

She smiled. "Everything was to your liking?"

"Everything was wonderful."

"And your case. It goes well?"

"So far, so good," he told her. Then he lowered his feet to the floor and stood up. "I'll walk you out."

He'd used Mrs. Leland for such events before and had come to like the matronly woman. She cooked a great meal and he could see that, however timidly, she found it exciting to do work for a private investigator.

"Would you like me to tell the young lady good-night, and the other gentleman? I could thank her for giving me the weekend off while he's there."

Max smiled. He'd told Mrs. Leland that she should pretend to work here full-time if the question came up when she was serving dinner. "That won't be necessary," he replied. "I mentioned it to him in passing already, but thanks for thinking of it."

When they reached the door, he pulled out his wallet and pushed a fifty-dollar bill into her hand. She raised her gaze to him, clearly astonished. "What's this for? I'll be sending my regular invoice to your office."

He grinned. "A tip. For services well rendered." He liked watching her eyes light up, and added, "Put this toward Joey's college expenses." He suspected that extra jobs such as this one were important to Mrs. Leland's family. She did housekeeping and cooking for a couple he knew and her husband worked in a factory, but Max imagined it was probably hard to make ends meet with three kids, the oldest a freshman in college.

"Well, thank you, Mr. Tate," she said, still smiling. "Thank you very much."

He opened the massive front door to let her out. "Have a safe drive home, Mrs. Leland. I'll be calling you the next time we need a nice meal."

He stood at the door and watched her get in her car

and drive away. Then he looked up at the sky, or more precisely, at the stars. You could see them here in the hills in much more abundance than from his place in the city. Too many lights in the city. Out here, it was easy to forget L.A. even existed. Warm night air swam around him and made him think, *Yep, I could get used to this.*

Oh, he'd never have the bucks for a place *this* ornate. But a man didn't need such extreme luxuries to be happy. Once he'd thought he did. Getting rich in Vegas had started to make him a little greedy, hence his Porsche. Since he'd made the decision to get out of the field and just run the company, though, he'd done some practical thinking about what it took to be happy.

There was no sin in owning some nice things, but he'd started figuring out that he was happiest being a middle-of-the-road kind of guy. A beer-and-pretzels guy who drove a Porsche. A corner-bar guy who wore Armani suits to work. He was achieving a happy medium. Finding the right balance of everything he needed to feel good when he got up in the morning and went to bed at night. And life was looking pretty good at the moment. *And a wife like this to share it all with? You've got the life, pal.*

Where had that thought come from?

But Max had no time to contemplate the answer because that's when Kimberly screamed.

4

MAX BOLTED toward the living room, ready to tear Carlo Coletti limb from sleazy limb.

To his surprise, he burst in only to find Carlo holding the stem of a broken glass, his shirt and jacket stained with dark liquid. "Oh, I'm so sorry, Carlo!" Kimberly said.

"What the hell happened?" Max asked.

They both looked up. "I'm so embarrassed," Kimberly said. "Carlo made a toast and I'm afraid I clinked our snifters too hard. I broke them both and got brandy all over poor Carlo."

Max's body flooded with relief, even though he could still feel his heart pounding against his ribs. Everything was okay here. Carlo wasn't attacking her. She wasn't hurt. Nothing was wrong.

"We'll have your clothes dry-cleaned, of course," she told Carlo as she bent to grab some small towels from a cabinet beneath the bar. Max was grateful she'd checked out the place so well and knew just where such things were kept.

She blotted a towel awkwardly against Carlo's chest, making Max cringe inside. Little snake. Even now, he was getting to have her touch him. Sort of, anyway. Thank God it was only sort of, or Max knew he'd be going crazy.

Max flinched. What was going on inside him? Why this crazed reaction to Kimberly doing her job? *Ego, ego, ego. Just keep telling yourself that, buddy.*

"Oh no," Carlo said then, "looks like the brandy splashed on you, too."

Max swung his gaze to Kimberly and saw that her chest was soaking wet...and Carlo was reaching for one of the dry towels.

No way, Max thought. No way in hell. He rushed forward and snatched the towel from Carlo's fist. "Darling," he said, "you really must be more careful." He tenderly pressed the towel against the low neckline of her dress, gently blotting the wetness.

He tensed when he felt her pull in her breath. He hadn't meant to startle her. He only wanted to protect her from Carlo. *Sorry.* He mouthed the word, his back to the slimy rat.

"It's all right." Her reply came in a breathy whisper.

Their gazes locked and he thought he saw passion in her eyes. Thought he felt her wanting him to touch her there, but without the towel. And he hoped he was wrong because this was no time for that. *No* time was the time for that. Not with them. Not anymore.

But her breasts were lush beneath him, the thin towel the only barrier between her flesh and his hands. The hell of it was that it would be easy to want her, so damn easy....

"Max," she said, loud enough that it shook him alert. "You'll need to get Carlo something else to wear."

"You're right," he replied, finally pulling the towel away from her and tossing it aside. "Why don't you go change, too, and I'll come with you and find something for Carlo."

"Sure," she said. Then she turned to Carlo, who once again had been ousted from a clandestine moment between Max and Kimberly and didn't look happy about it. "Relax and help yourself to something else in the liquor cabinet, Carlo."

As they exited the room, Max planted his hand at the small of Kimberly's back where her little black dress hugged her curves. But as they climbed the stairs, he thought back to her scream, and to the way it had run through him like a sword.

An overreaction on her part, big time. That hadn't been an I-broke-a-glass-and-made-a-mess kind of scream, but an I'm-being-molested one. For the first time since it had happened, he had the chance to start getting angry. At the top of the stairs, he grabbed her wrist and spun her to face him. "Don't ever do that again," he snapped, though he worked to keep his tone low enough that Carlo wouldn't hear.

Her eyes looked darker now, more brown, in the dim lighting of the upstairs hall. "Do what?"

"Don't scream like that unless you mean it."

"I meant it."

But he kept right on going, his anger reaching a fever pitch now. "Do you know how badly that scared me? Do you know what I thought was happening to you in there? You don't scream like that unless something's really wrong, Kimberly. Got it?"

Got it, she was supposed to reply, but she didn't.

Instead, her voice came out hushed and snide. "Look, something *was* wrong and breaking those glasses wasn't an accident. The guy's hand was lingering dangerously close to my breasts, and he was ready to pounce. I had the feeling I might not be able to hold him off. So I went with my impulse and slammed my glass into his. And for your information, I kind of felt like I needed you in there. You abandoned me without warning. I know this is my job, but your job is to be there if I need you, remember? So I'll scream whenever I damn well feel like screaming. Now, do *you* got it?"

Damn, Max thought. He'd had no idea Carlo would make a move like that so fast. She was right, he should've been there. But he'd misjudged Carlo's technique. He'd also been selfish, not wanting to have to watch the jerk get close to her.

He took a deep breath. "You're right. I'm sorry, Brandt. I should've been keeping an eye on things."

She was still looking at him as if she wanted to kill him, until finally she turned and stalked toward the master suite. He started to follow, when suddenly she stopped and faced him, one finger in the air. "This doesn't mean I can't handle the guy, Tate."

"I didn't say it did."

"Because I can. I can do my job, and you'd better not start thinking I can't."

"Brandt, I didn't—"

"I'm not the same woman you knew before, Tate. I'm no shrinking violet. I'm a lot tougher than before, a lot more capable. Got it?"

What could he say to all that? Judging by what he'd seen so far, it seemed a completely valid self-assessment. "Got it."

KIMBERLY STEPPED from the oversize shower, glad to feel clean. Clean of the brandy. Clean of Carlo's disgusting touches. After the brandy incident, she'd been more than ready to call it a day.

Beyond the bathroom door, she thought she heard Max come in. "Tate, is that you?"

"Yeah, it's me."

Next, she stepped into the enormous closet, which was attached to the bathroom, looking through her own contributions to the clothing that hung there. She pulled one of the nighties she'd brought from a satin-covered hanger. She was more than a little nervous about putting it on, but worrying was useless at this point. Of course, had she known the kind of reaction she'd end up having to Max, she'd have definitely brought a wider variety of sleepwear. As it was, she was stuck wearing the short, yellow, rather *thin* night-gown.

She changed into it with her back to the mirror, afraid of how revealing she might suddenly find it to be. Whether or not worrying was useless, it was also seemingly impossible to prevent. Even without looking in the mirror, she knew this thing was practically see-through. What on earth had she been thinking when she packed? Bring sexy clothes, Max had told her. *That's* what she'd been thinking. So she'd ravaged her closets and drawers for anything that seemed sexy. She'd had little time to measure practicality and now she had to walk out into the bedroom—the bedroom they had to *share*—and face him in *this!*

If she were to do this, she'd need to distract herself and...just act normal. That's it, she thought. Act normal and so will Max. It was that simple.

"Is Carlo all settled in for the night?" she asked through the door. A good, sensible, *normal* kind of question.

"I showed him to one of the guest rooms, gave him

some sweats to wear, and he went back down to watch TV," Max replied on the other side. "He seemed terribly disappointed that you didn't come back down with me."

"Yeah, well, I've had about as much Carlo Coletti as I can stand for one night." And Max couldn't say she hadn't earned her pay tonight.

"You mind if I ask you a question, out of curiosity?" Max asked then.

"Sure." She returned to the bathroom and started removing her makeup. This acting-normal stuff was going well, she thought, even spurring conversation.

"After seeing the way Carlo behaves around you," Max said, "I find myself wondering... Why would all these women sleep with this raunchy guy? Frankly, I'm baffled. Can you shed any light on that?"

Kimberly decided to share the thoughts she'd had on the same issue earlier. "He's sort of a handsome man, Tate."

"He is?"

She smiled, amused at how shocked he sounded. "Well, yeah. Sure, he's a jerk and an obvious lech, but if a woman were, say, suffering from low self-esteem or in a bad marriage or something, maybe she would choose not to see Carlos's bad points. Having a guy fall all over you and give you compliments might make you feel special or something."

It took Max a minute to reply. "What about you? He didn't make *you* feel special or something, did he?"

He almost sounded jealous. *Almost.* But his question, Kimberly decided, more likely stemmed from fear that she'd soften toward Carlo and botch things up. He was afraid this was just another version of the Carpenter case all over again.

Still, she kept her cool and answered without getting upset. "No, he makes *me* feel creepy, but I'm just not sure all women would realize what kind of a guy he is. I know it seems obvious to you—and to me, too—but a lot of women thrive on flattery, Tate. If a woman feels alone or neglected or something, well, I could see it happening."

"Hmm." That was all he said. So she didn't know what he thought of her response, if he was out there doubting her abilities again or something.

But at the moment, she had other things to worry about. She was done taking off her makeup and was still standing in front of the mirror when... Yikes! This nightie *was* revealing!

Act normal, she reminded herself. Just act normal.

I'm coming out now. She thought about announcing that through the door, but that *wouldn't* be very normal, would it? So she held her tongue and prepared to open the door. Her stomach filled with more of those grenade-wielding butterflies that she'd become acquainted with since seeing Max again. Oh boy, this wasn't gonna be easy.

Kimberly took a deep breath and pulled the door open, casually entering the bedroom. Max lay on the bed wearing a pair of white drawstring lounging pants, no shirt. He looked *so* good. It didn't help her nervousness one bit.

She walked around to the other side of the bed, thankfully unnoticed until Max looked up from the magazine he was flipping through.

"Is that what you brought to sleep in?" She could feel his eyes on her, his expression practically aghast.

She swallowed and forced herself to look at him. "Well," she explained, "I didn't think ratty pajamas would really fit my new image."

"He's not *sleeping* with us, Brandt."

She pulled back the covers. "You said before that it was possible he'd sneak around in the night or something weird like that. I thought he might see me."

"Too *much* of you."

His eyes were still on her, as if glued to her and his tone almost made Kimberly think... No, it couldn't be. But then, there *had* been that kiss. That soul-stirring, weaken-your-knees kiss. He'd even used his tongue. She knew she shouldn't say it, knew it was a stupid, crazy thought, but she was tired and when she got tired she sometimes couldn't think clearly enough to stop herself from saying stupid, crazy things. "I thought letting him see too much of me was the idea here. You sound jealous, Tate."

He tilted his head as if to say, *You've got to be kidding.* "Don't be ludicrous. And the idea is to be friendly to the guy, Brandt, not incite him to attack you."

Kimberly chose not to reply. Instead, she slid beneath the sheets—made of some kind of fabulous silk that felt glorious next to her skin—wondering if that was what *Max* wanted to do, attack her. He would say no, of course, but his eyes said yes.

Then she remembered. She'd never been able to read his eyes. he was always able to hide his feelings, no matter what was going on. What looked like lust to her was just as likely annoyance, or maybe even some kind of disgust. Besides, when would she get it through her thick head, once and for all? Everything Max did in front of Carlo was pretend and everything he did away from Carlo was belligerent. Even if he *had* tolerated her outrage in the hall, she'd been justified about that and he knew it. Any way you sliced it, it was still all business.

She only wished it were that way for *her*—all business. She wished she saw Max as only a co-worker, because how she was going to sleep next to him like this, she didn't know. She shook her head in frustration against the fluffy silk-covered pillow beneath her, then pulled the covers up over her breasts, pressing her bare arms to her sides above the sheets. *Think normal,* she told herself.

Oh, who was she kidding? This was about as far from normal as any situation she'd ever been in. What she felt for Max—in every sensuously charged fiber of her body at the moment—was far from normal, too. She had a feeling it was going to be a very long night.

"Ready for lights out?" Max asked.

Next to him, she nodded. Max set his magazine on the bedside table, then reached up and flipped the switch that darkened the room. He settled on his back, thinking, *What a relief.* But then, not really. The only relief was that the lights were out and he could quit trying to look so unaffected by the sight of her. Yet affected he was. He'd seen her nipples through that silky yellow fabric. A dark, rosy color, they'd been poking prominently against the front of her sexy little gown. What had she been thinking, wearing *that* to bed with him?

Well, the answer didn't matter. What mattered was that the picture of those taut, rose-colored buds was planted firmly in his mind now and he knew there was no way he would quit thinking about Kimberly any time soon.

He wanted desperately to roll over and touch her breasts. He wanted to kiss their enticing peaks. He remembered her breasts clearly—*too* clearly. Round and soft and very sensitive, they'd filled his hands perfectly. She had nipples that beaded instantly when he touched them, that hardened into tiny pebbles against his tongue.

God, it would be easy, *so* easy...but no longer just easy to want her. The fact was, he already did. He didn't want to feel that way, he wanted to keep right on fighting it, but he was hard as a rock beneath the covers and there was no denying *that*. Now it would be easy to roll over onto her, to plant another of those full, deep kisses on her mouth, to take those two sweet mounds of flesh into his eager hands, to press his aching hardness into the place where he knew she was soft and warm.

Get hold of yourself, Tate. You're on the job here, for God's sake. Quit acting like a fourteen-year-old boy who just saw his first naked woman.

He rolled over away from her to be sure he didn't make a tent of the covers. She'd been right earlier—this *was* inappropriate, them sleeping next to each other. But he hadn't planned on feeling this way, hadn't really expected it at all, so he hadn't foreseen this problem.

Damn it, on top of everything else, she smelled good, too. Like the dusting powder he remembered she loved—a sexy, musky scent that always made him think of summertime heat. She must still put it on each night before she went to bed. How would he last the night smelling her like this, remembering the sight of her breasts through that sheer little gown, wanting to feel her and taste her?

He rolled onto his back again and then he rolled once more to face her, to watch her sleeping in the faint glow of the security lights that shone dimly through the windows. She was beautiful. More now than before. Earlier, in that dress made for sin, she'd looked beyond hot, beyond steamy. But now, like this, she was just a plain natural beauty, simple with her bed-tousled hair and lips half parted in sleep, the lipstick gone to leave them a familiar color, like slightly faded berries.

Either way, it didn't matter how she looked—the lust he felt for her was intense. He knew that if he stayed in this bed much longer, he'd be reaching out his hand beneath the sheets and...

Come on, Tate, shake this off now. You're a professional. Act like it.

Finally, Max pushed back the covers and got out of bed. He couldn't sleep here and not have her. He took his pillow and made his way to one of the chairs across the room by the fireplace, where he'd just have to suffer until morning.

KIMBERLY AWOKE to the songs of birds beyond the balcony door and was surprised to be waking at all— she'd not expected to ever fall asleep last night.

She rolled slowly in Max's direction, then cautiously eased her eyes open.

He was gone!

She sat up in bed, startled, but she quickly spotted

him across the room, curled impossibly in one of the chairs by the fireplace, one leg stretched across the marble table.

Her heart sank a little at the sight. Sleeping next to him had been difficult, but that didn't mean she'd wanted him to leave. Just being close to him—whether or not they touched—made her feel so...alive.

Oh well, she thought, slumping back against her pillow. So much for feeling alive. She'd not imagined it would bother him so much to sleep next to her that he'd actually feel compelled to get up and go away. He must harbor even worse feelings for her than she realized. Maybe even worse feelings than *he* understood. After all, it had been his plan that they share the room and the bed.

She rolled back over on her side and shut her eyes tight, holding back the tears that threatened to leak free. A P.I. didn't cry, especially not one who was determined to show her old boss she was worthy of her job. *Be tough, Kimberly,* she commanded herself. She'd had no trouble being surer, cockier these past three years since parting ways with Max. She'd had to be. She'd had to let her personality take on new dimensions in order to keep her emotions out of her work. But Max... Well, he was enough to bring all her old feelings rushing back, and she didn't know what she could possibly do to stop it.

THREE HOURS LATER, Kimberly lay in her bikini, stretched out next to the pool in a fabulous lounge chair. Next to her, the water sparkled in aqua splendor beneath the sun. Potted palms dotted the area, vibrant summer flowers in bright yellows and hot pinks lining the perimeter. Teak lawn furniture sat scattered randomly, the tables covered with enormous turquoise umbrellas, and hidden speakers sent music wafting over the backyard to make the scene complete. Kimberly lay back and sighed with the grandeur of it all. L.A. wasn't the Caribbean, but sometimes it came close.

Another heavenly aspect of the moment was that she was alone in her sunny paradise, at least for now. Carlo and Max had gone out to get steaks for the grill. She desperately needed this private time to regroup from everything that had already happened...and to prepare for everything yet to take place.

For one thing, she'd grown suddenly squeamish about having Carlo's eyes on her in a bikini. She didn't normally have qualms over hiding her body, but it was different when a man was looking at you like *that*. She thought of that lecherous quality she'd sensed in him instantly, and she found herself hoping that Max would be around for the duration of their sunning and swimming.

Then again, she was practically as squeamish about Max right now, only in a different way. She still felt embarrassed that he'd left the bed and she even wondered if he'd somehow been able to feel her wanting him so badly. They'd not discussed it this morning. She'd fallen back asleep and by the time she reawakened, Max had showered and dressed. He'd conveniently stepped out onto the balcony while she scurried to the bathroom, all the more aware of what she still wore.

She released a long sigh into the balmy air, remembering how she'd promised herself that she wouldn't give in to her desire for him. Yet that kiss before dinner last night had quickly done her in and now she felt helpless. It would be good to refocus on her original goals for this job, just as she'd thought about this morning. She needed to show Max that she wouldn't let him down, which meant she needed to be tough. And she needed to survive being near him without going crazy with lust.

A tall order, but she could do it. She *would* do it.

Only she would do it later. Right now, this was *her* time. She planned to bask in the sun, and the luxury of it all. To clear her mind and get reenergized. Kimberly closed her eyes and let the soft sounds of the music fill her, let the warmth of the sun lull her into relaxation.

MAX WAS GLAD he'd noticed a supermarket nearby as he and Kimberly had driven to the mansion yesterday, or else he wouldn't have known where to go for steaks. Carlo wasn't the sharpest knife in the cutting block, but even *he* might have found it suspicious if Max didn't know where to buy groceries.

Now he and Carlo were meandering the aisles together, and Max covered his lack of store knowledge by explaining that Mrs. Leland did most of their shopping. Anything else they needed, Kimberly usually picked up.

"Gorgeous woman, that Kimberly," Carlo said. Max just wanted to shake his head at the guy. How many times had Carlo made the same comment since he'd met her? *Get a new line, Carlo,* he wanted to say. *Remember you're talking to her husband.* But Carlo seemed so completely taken by her that if he had any sense at all, it had obviously vanished.

"Yes, she certainly is," Max said, his stock reply. He spotted the meat counter in the back of the sprawling store. "This way."

"Bet she's something in bed," Carlo snickered under his breath.

Was this guy serious? Max wasn't even sure if Carlo had intended him to hear that, but either way, what a total clod! Under any other circumstances, Max would have punched the jerk in the mouth, but that wasn't on the agenda here. *Stay cool. Play dumb. That's your role, annoying as it is.* Instead, he gave a throaty, knowing laugh and said, "I don't divulge trade secrets."

Although he smiled to himself and knew that if he did tell Carlo about Kimberly, he'd have said that she was outstanding in bed, that making love to her was, in fact, a sublime experience. Not that he could speak from *recent* experience, but those kinds of memories didn't fade.

Max ordered the steaks from the butcher while Carlo went off in search of beer. While he waited for the meat to be wrapped, he found his mind drifting back to what had happened last night, or more precisely, to what had *not* happened. Apparently, Kimberly didn't even have to be doing anything in bed to drive him wild—just sleeping near her was enough to make him crazed. He shook his head at the insanity of it.

Only now was it occurring to him that he'd been so in heat over her that he'd lain there obsessing over it, not even thinking about Carlo or the case or the fact that they were all under the same roof. Carlo had been lying in the next room still planning to rob them—Max knew that much. So, in effect, Carlo had been on the job and Max hadn't. Kimberly had completely taken over his mind. *Not exactly good form, Tate,* he berated himself.

Well, it was just a damn good thing he'd gotten out of bed. One thing was for sure, this had been a wake-up call. He couldn't let her keep distracting him. The job depended on it. And his client was depending on it. From now on, he'd shape up and take control of this thing. No more juvenile reactions. No more thinking with his pants.

As Carlo returned, a twelve-pack of beer tucked under each arm, Max realized it was back to work. That meant doing just what would reel old Carlo in—turning things back toward his "wife." He decided to drop a line that would come in handy later when they put the sting in motion.

"Kimberly will really enjoy grilling outside this afternoon," he said as the butcher handed him the steaks. "We have that huge area for entertaining, but with just the two of us, and me being so busy at work, we don't make much use of it."

"Spend a lot of time at work, do you?"

Max held back his smile. Carlo had taken his bait perfectly. This was too easy. "Yeah. I'm stuck there late a lot of nights. Sometimes I even get called in on weekends. I know Kimberly gets tired of spending so much time on her own."

"Weekends, too, huh? That's rough. Happen very often?"

Max pretended to be concentrating on the vast array of snack chips he'd turned to study. "Mmm, yeah, pretty often."

Carlo's eyes widened earnestly. "Well, I hope you don't get called in this afternoon 'cause I'm looking forward to these steaks," he said with a smile. "But if you do..."

Max scooped up a bag of corn chips. "Yeah?"

"Well, at least Kimberly won't be left alone. I'll be there to keep her company."

Max grinned and even patted Carlo on the back. "I guess that's true. And I'm sure Kimberly is enjoying your visit."

"Oh?"

Max played it off as nothing. "Well, it's quiet in that big house, even when I *am* home. I just get the idea sometimes that...well, that she might like a change of pace, you know?"

Carlo let his smile deepen, clearly reading into the words exactly what Max wanted him to. Max had decided earlier that imaginary call into the office wouldn't come until tomorrow. It wasn't that he wanted to stretch this thing out—it already seemed interminably long—but he didn't want to be obvious by rushing it. Carlo had spent four days with Max's client before he'd made the move to seduce her and steal her jewelry. Of course, maybe his client's husband wasn't as blind and encouraging as Max was, but one day just seemed too soon. Two would be better.

"That reminds me," he added. "Kimberly and I were talking last night and we both thought, why not invite Carlo to stay the whole weekend, let those paint fumes settle a while? What do you say?"

Carlo's smile now stretched from ear to ear. "Sounds great!"

Thought it would, Max wanted to mumble, but he held it in.

The two men began making their way to the check-out when Max stopped. "Hang on a minute," he said to Carlo, and then went to the aisle where they kept the wine products and grabbed a carton of tropical-flavored wine coolers. It had just hit him that Kimberly had never been much of a beer drinker, but he knew she was fond of wine.

Upon returning to the house, Max immediately suggested that Carlo go back to his place and pick up enough clothes for a couple of days.

"I'll heat up the grill while you're gone," Max said, waving as Carlo departed.

Once Carlo was finally out of sight, Max turned away, glad to let the smile fade, glad to quit acting for a few minutes. That's why he'd insisted Carlo go with him to the store. Besides not wanting to leave Kimberly alone with the guy, he wanted to make sure she had an ample break before resuming her role. Now he'd discovered he needed a break, too. It would be good to have the creep gone for a little while.

Max went inside and put the steaks and drinks in the refrigerator, then located the plates and utensils he'd need for grilling, gathering them on the counter. After that, he moved toward the French doors in the back, where Kimberly was probably relaxing by the pool.

He opened one of the doors and stopped dead in his tracks. Yep, Kimberly was by the pool, all right. She lay there in glorious, sensuous abandon, her arms lifted over her head, her body stretched across the chair like a cat sunning itself.

He'd forgotten how good she looked in a bikini. This one was bold with a floral design that suited the vibrant surroundings. But he wasn't really looking at the bikini. He was looking at what was in it.

Kimberly was no twig—she had a perfect hourglass shape, all slender, all curves, and all of it looking incredibly touchable. His mind drifted back in time to what he knew about those curves, to how they felt in his hands. Touching her was like touching a work of art, her body soft and malleable.

He was getting hard again just watching her. Which was not good. Hadn't he just told himself this kind of crap had to stop? Hadn't he just realized he was putting everything in jeopardy by letting his body take over his mind?

He ran one hand back through his hair and kept gaping at her. She was asleep, which somehow made this seem all the more bad. She didn't even know what she was doing to him—she was completely innocent—and all the logic and reasoning in the world wasn't gonna make the hardness in his shorts disappear. Damn it, he was only flesh and blood. And she was...beyond tempting. Just look at her, he thought. Perfection in the sun.

Then he remembered how she always burned in the sun, how she never took the time to put on sunscreen, always so anxious to bask in the rays, to just soak it all up.

So he stepped outside and went to the small pool house across the way. Inside, he found sunscreen—a vast array of the stuff—so he chose a medium protection, and exited without a plan.

Just give it to her, he told himself. *Just wake her up, fill her in on what she missed with Carlo, and give her the damn sunscreen.*

But inside he was trembling. Trembling with how badly he wanted to touch her. Wondering, would she welcome it, would she want it, too, his hands on her body?

Max knew things were out of control now. He knew he was way too turned on to push down his desire for her, way too turned on to do anything but act on it. He knew it was suicide, in more ways than he cared to acknowledge. But he couldn't keep himself from going to her, not even for one more second.

He walked across the patio and gazed down on her, all the heat in his veins making his entire body pulse with anticipation.

Then he kneeled next to her...and reached out to touch her.

5

IN KIMBERLY'S DREAM, Max was touching her.

His fingers drifted over her bare stomach, moving in slow wide circles. He was rubbing something—lotion—onto her, making her hot skin feel moist and slick beneath the sun's heat. It was a good dream.

She pulled her breath in with a slow hiss when he ventured farther down, moving his touch over her belly button and lower, to the edge of her bikini bottom. She bit her lip when his fingertips slid inside. Oh yes, this was a *very* good dream.

When he slid them back out, she suffered a small stab of disappointment. But after a wet dollop of lotion connected with her thigh, she began to think sleepily, *Oh, what if this isn't a dream? What if Max is really touching...?*

She tried to grab on to the thought, but half sleep kept her from thinking clearly, from waking fully. She finally found the strength to ease her eyes open then, and she found...dear God, Max bending over her, applying lotion to her legs. "Oh," she breathed.

Max looked up and their gazes met, but he didn't stop massaging the lotion. He worked it into her calf now, his touch deep and slow, like the penetrating caress of a lover.

"Didn't want you to burn," he finally whispered.

"Where is..."

"Not here."

"Oh, then it's..."

"Just you and me. For now."

"Mmm." She bit her lip as his fingers plied deeply into her thigh, moving back up her leg. It felt so good. *Too* good.

"Close your eyes, babe," he whispered.

She didn't argue or protest, just did what he asked. She closed her eyes and let him keep touching her, and touching her, and touching her.

He used both hands, smoothing the lotion into her other leg, down her thigh, over her knee and down her calf. Then he slid his hands warmly back up, still rubbing, massaging, making her tingle with heated desire as they came higher, closer to where she longed for his sweet touch.

Max pulled away then and shifted his ministrations to a new place, rubbing lotion onto her shoulders and slowly down each arm. Kimberly lay there drinking it all in, each sexy touch, each sliver of excitement that it injected into her soul.

Then his fingers were near her neck, smoothing, pressing in small rhythmic circles, working their way down one strap of her bikini top, moving onto the exposed ridge of her breast, fingertips reaching just past the top's edge, sending her desire to a fever pitch. She bit her lip in response to the throbbing sensations below. She wanted him to touch her more, *everywhere*. Wanted him to slide one hand into her top, another into her bottoms. Wanted to move against him and seek her pleasure and explode for him in wild release.

Her lips were trembling now. *Kiss me*, she thought. *Oh please, Max, kiss me.*

But Max, who had always been a slow and very thorough lover, continued in the same pattern, his fingers now leaving the valley between her breasts and gliding up onto the curve of the other. Kimberly bit her lip harder to keep from whimpering, to keep from begging.

Her heart beat a frantic cadence when he moved his caresses back down her body, the cool lotion being smoothed into the skin at her hips and the tops of her thighs. So close, so achingly near to the center of her desire. "Oh, Max..." She hadn't meant to utter it, but it had come naturally with her escalating need.

"I didn't get around the edges of your suit before." He spoke in a husky timbre, making it clear to them both that this was not the real reason his touch lingered in this particular area. She opened her eyes and their gazes connected. "Should I stop, babe?"

She let out a heavy breath she hadn't realized she was holding, then gave her head a short shake. An emphatic *no*.

His dark, sexy eyes narrowed on her with a heat so intense that it might have frightened her coming from anyone else. But it didn't frighten her with Max. *Nothing* frightened her with Max. She loved him, and she wanted him to touch her so badly that she could taste it.

He slid the tips of his fingers beneath the thin strip of material at her hip. She sucked in her breath again, wanting this sweet, horrible teasing to end, wanting him to touch her *there*. *Now*. "Max," she whispered. "Please."

She heard his labored breathing above her and let her eyes fall shut. His fingertips were moving, sliding ever so slowly, ever so hotly, getting nearer, nearer, until she wanted to scream. She realized that she was gripping the arms of the chair as if holding on for dear life, and she was panting wildly. Then his strong fingers moved over and down through the small thatch of hair and slid warm into—

His hand was suddenly gone.

"Damn," he said.

Kimberly's eyes bolted open and she raised her head. "Max?"

He stood above her, looking down. "I just heard a car door. He's back."

"Oh," she sighed in utter disbelief. *He was back? How could this be? How could it happen?*

They stared at each other for a long, awkward moment, thrust unpleasantly back to the reality of why they were here. Kimberly longed to say something, anything, to make this seem less strange and uncomfortable, to make it seem normal and right, but she couldn't find any words.

"I'd...better go meet him," Max finally said. And then he was gone, disappearing through the French doors, leaving Kimberly alone to hold back tears of frustration.

Oh damn it! she thought. Now Carlo was here and the role-playing would begin again. She had to be ready for him and she had to be tough and she had to be that way *right now*.

She'd be damned if they were both going to come back out and find her lying here looking scared and bereft and nervous. She refused to let Carlo come upon her stretched-out body and gawk at her and feel all the things she wanted to make only Max feel.

So she rose from the lounge chair and dove into the pool, and tried to let the cool water swallow all her frustrations.

"HERE YOU GO, babe. Medium-well, just the way you like it." Max set a sizzling-hot steak in front of Kimberly on one of the teak tables on the patio.

"Thanks," she said, returning his smile, although she wondered if his smile was real or fake. All the lines were getting blurred.

She really did like her steaks medium-well, and he hadn't had to ask. But considering what had happened just before Carlo had arrived, Kimberly could hardly concentrate on how much she liked it that he remembered another detail about her. There were bigger things on her mind, like Max himself and the strange sensations that rushed through her still—passion tainted with embarrassment. Or was that embarrassment tainted with passion?

Temper that with the ghoulish feeling of having her breasts ogled by Carlo while she cut into her steak, and things got icky. She'd just figured out that it wasn't merely Carlo's blatant lust that bothered her—she'd had problems with men like him before, men who saw women as nothing more than sexual objects. It was dealing with this at the same time as she tried to deal with wanting Max that made things so hard. It was difficult putting up the tough wall of *un*emotion required to deal with guys like Carlo while she was immersed in her very *emotional* response to Max.

She gave her head a slight shake, recalling the encounter they'd shared over the sunscreen. That was the last thing she'd have expected from Max, especially after last night when he'd left the bed she slept in. She couldn't have been more shocked.

"Pass the salt, will you please, Kimberly?" The voice belonged to Carlo and the move required a long reach on her part, toward the other side of the table and then back to him. His eyes drank in her every move. *Pig*, she muttered to herself as she handed the shaker to him and watched him sprinkle only the tiniest bit on his food.

Under the table then, Carlo leaned his knee into hers. Her body instinctively froze. Instincts also told her to shift her legs away from his and toward Max, who was just now taking a seat on the other side of her at the round table, but she knew leaning her legs away would be the wrong move, casewise. It was time to start being a little more responsive to the suspect, a little more inviting. She'd not exactly been pushing him away up to this point, but if Carlo was to make his play sometime this weekend, she needed to start altering her actions and letting him know she liked him. The thought nearly made her gag, but it was what the job called for.

So she forced herself to leave her knees where they were, disgusting as it was. She even tossed him a coy little smile. She didn't look at Max to see if he noticed, but she was glad he was there, just the same. And she was glad he'd be in the closet when Carlo tried to seduce her, too. She still hadn't figured out the sunscreen encounter—what it might mean, where it left them now—but she needed Max's protection with this guy. And besides, he owed it to her. After all, it was him and his amorous attention that had left her feeling so volatile right now.

She let Carlo's knees touch hers for two minutes, maybe more, then moved. That was enough—a good, bold, teaser-type invitation—and it was all she could stand.

After she finished her meal, Kimberly lay her napkin on the table and leaned back in her seat. She'd gotten a slight cramp in her neck, probably from falling asleep in the lounge chair earlier. Emotionally tired, sated from the large meal and practically ready for another nap, she let her eyes fall shut and rolled her neck slowly, trying to work out the kink. Bad move.

"Here, let me help you with that." It was Carlo, of course, rising from his chair and moving behind her to massage her shoulders. "I took a class on this," he went on, "so I know just what to do to make it feel better." She'd completely forgotten what a blatant opportunist the little skunk was.

But she knew when to make a situation work for *her*, too. "Thanks, Carlo. That feels wonderful." She let the last word drag out in a sensuous sort of way she knew he would appreciate. And she put up her little emotional wall that allowed the creep to touch her without her wanting to turn around and strangle him.

Yes, lead him on, she thought. *Make him think you want him. Let's get this show on the road.* Because the sooner the mission was accomplished, the sooner she could go home and get off this crazy roller-coaster ride with Max once and for all.

Being around him again was fantastic, but *so* confusing. If anything was going to start back up between them, it would happen much easier after this case was through.

Then she caught Max staring at her, one elbow propped on the arm of his chair, his chin balanced on a loose fist. As usual, she couldn't read his expression. Anyone else in the world—yes. She'd gotten much better at that sort of thing in their time apart. Frank had schooled her on it this past year. But not Max and those warm brown pools of his. They stayed as cloaked and mysterious to her as ever.

Still, she looked back, trying her hardest not to show him any emotion, either—her confusion and frustration from what had happened earlier, her disgust over being touched by this thief. They exchanged what she thought of as a blank, yet somehow serious, stare for the length of Carlo's grating massage.

Max didn't like Carlo being so touchy-feely with Kimberly. He hadn't liked it last night, either, but at least then she'd been wearing a little more clothing. He knew from very recent experience just how accessible she was at the moment, just how easy it was to reach beneath the fabric. He hated having her in such a vulnerable position with this guy and not being able to intervene without blowing the case.

He wanted to kick himself for giving in to his own wants when he'd come upon her sunning, and for having had to leave them both so on the edge of ecstasy. *Man, what bad timing Carlo had,* Max thought, shaking his head. Things had been incredibly hot, tension-filled, but in a good way. In an intense way. She'd wanted him to touch her as much as he'd wanted to.

At the moment, he also kind of wanted to kill Kimberly for sitting there letting *Carlo* touch her so much, encouraging it with her little moans of pleasure, giggling when the jerk made a stupid joke.

It's her job, you idiot, he reminded himself. But did she really have to be *that* encouraging? Something about it made Max's stomach churn.

So, she really thought this guy was handsome? Seemed crazy to Max, but that's what she'd told him last night. Handsome. *Compared to me?* he'd even been tempted to say. Now he was glad he hadn't.

He might have asked himself how he could account for all his feelings if he hadn't been so busy holding Kimberly's gaze, trying to see what she was really feeling. But at the moment her expression was surprisingly masked, surprisingly unreadable, which bugged him more than he could understand.

HOURS LATER, Max stood in the kitchen in his swim trunks, his back against one of the French doors, arms crossed in front of him. He watched Kimberly moving around the room, putting things away, running food scraps through the disposal, scouring grilling utensils over the sink, all the while still in her bikini, perky as hell. Carlo was upstairs showering, but that didn't diminish Max's annoyance. After all, she'd spent the whole afternoon flirting with Carlo.

Max cringed at the awful memory of her sitting on the edge of the pool and Carlo pulling on her ankle, trying to get her to come into the water with him. Before it was done, the slimeball's hands had climbed up her calf to the back of her knee. She'd giggled the whole time, saying, "You'd better stop it, Carlo," although it had clearly been in jest. Max had simply stood by watching, getting angrier with each passing minute.

Yes, it was the role she'd been hired to play. But did she have to make him look so dumb and blind? And did she have to do that pretty, lighthearted little giggle so damn much?

And now here she was, still flitting around in her bikini inside the house. Soon enough Carlo would be back down here and Max had the bad feeling that if he turned his back for a minute, Carlo would be all over her, and maybe inside that bikini, too. Sure, he was here to protect her, but in his opinion, she needed to exercise a little self-preservation, as well.

Now she was putting away the plates she'd just washed and dried, reaching up into an overhead cabinet on her tiptoes. She arched her back, making herself taller and sticking out her cute little bottom in the process. A nice view. Too nice. One he was sure Carlo would enjoy if he were here.

Only when Kimberly closed the cabinet door and looked around for her next chore did she seem to notice his disgruntled look. "What's wrong?"

"Maybe you should put some more clothes on," he replied evenly.

The words took Kimberly aback and made her chest tighten. His tone implied that she was doing something wrong here. She refrained from responding, not quite sure what to say in the midst of her surprise, but gave him a look of warning that dared him to go on.

He took the dare, although he kept his voice low. "I think it's safe to say that the bikini has more than done its job with Carlo. You can cover yourself up a little better now."

Oh boy. Was he serious? Kimberly tried to keep from fuming inside, but it was hard to push it down. At this point in the game, she had no intention of taking any crap from Max. She kept her voice low, as well, when she said, "What's the problem here?"

"No problem," he answered in a gruff whisper. "But I didn't exactly see why you had to let him touch you so damn much all day."

"Hmm, let's see," she replied sarcastically, a fingertip at her bottom lip. "I'm supposed to make the guy think I want to have sex with him. I'm supposed to make him think I'm completely willing to do that, so I didn't run screaming from him when he started to touch me. Silly me, what *could* I have been thinking?"

He narrowed his eyes in response to her sarcasm. "I hadn't envisioned it including a lot of touching, that's all."

"You didn't envision touching? Well, for someone who didn't envision touching, *you've* certainly been doing enough of it. In fact, I was beginning to think that was my sole purpose here—to be touched and fondled by any man within reach."

He took a step toward her. "What's that supposed to mean?"

Kimberly let out a deep breath. She couldn't believe it! He was actually going to act as if he didn't know what she was talking about. "Well, in case you weren't paying attention, Carlo's not the only man in this house who's had trouble keeping his hands off me. After all, what was that kiss you gave me at the door last night?"

He stiffened. "That was professional. To help him view you in a sexual light."

"Oh, and then what was that at the pool today when he wasn't even around?"

He let out a heavy breath, and his expression shifted from anger to bitter honesty. "That? That was lust, Kimberly."

Lust. The word halted her in place. She lusted for him, too, but what she felt for him went deeper than mere lust. She *loved* him. Kimberly knew he didn't love her back, knew too much had happened for him to ever love her, but lust, at the moment, made her feel empty inside. She said nothing, only blinked to make sure she didn't start to cry.

"What the hell am I supposed to feel here?" he boomed at her then. "First last night, seeing you in that dress—"

"You told me to look that way!"

"You're right, I did. But I sure didn't tell you to come to bed wearing a tiny see-through nightgown. And then today, that bikini. I know, you're supposed to wear that, too. But seeing so much of your body just finally got to me, all right? It was unprofessional and I know it. So sue me. But it takes two to tango, doesn't it? You weren't exactly fighting me off, were you?"

Kimberly had heard enough. She turned and stalked away from him, out of the kitchen and down the massive hall. So he lusted for her and he thought what she felt for him was a simple matter of two bodies drawn to each other by something as meaningless as chemistry, too. She entered the bathroom, shut the door and let herself cry, hating herself for the tears even as she set them free.

Well, this would end *now*, she decided adamantly. She'd change out of her bathing suit as soon as she exited the bathroom. And if she had to, she would wear a potato sack to bed tonight, but she certainly wouldn't wear another of the nighties she'd unwittingly packed. She'd do nothing to tempt him that wasn't completely necessary to the role. She'd do this job, catch this creep, collect her pay and be gone.

She'd started thinking that being back around Max was wonderful, but she'd been wrong. It was painful and she wanted it to end as soon as possible.

Drying her tears with a tissue, Kimberly composed herself and came out, ready to be in character if she confronted Carlo. Then she made her way to the stairs, and to the master suite, ready to change into something Max might find more acceptable now that he was suddenly the clothing police.

UPON COMING BACK downstairs in a short, shape-flattering but amply covering yellow linen dress, Kimberly was met by Max and informed that their guest was sitting out on the patio enjoying what remained of the day's sun. Then he grabbed her hand and led her down the hall to the office, shutting the door behind them.

At first Kimberly feared Max was going to continue berating her about her bikini, or perhaps find fault in what she wore now, despite its being the most conservative thing she'd brought. Instead, he turned to face her, leaning back against the desk in a stylish button-up shirt and a slightly faded pair of blue jeans, and said, "Let's talk strategy."

"All right." She herself was more than eager to talk strategy at this point—it seemed the only safe subject between them.

"I told Carlo I wanted to take you both out for a casual dinner tonight. I saw a little bistro earlier that looked nice. I figured I'd use the dinner as a chance to try to find out more about him. He's pretty tight-lipped about himself, but we might get something. We could also try bringing up the jewelry again. Maybe we can wheedle some hint about where he's stashing or selling the jewels he steals. A long shot, but worth a try."

"Okay. I'll follow your lead."

"After that, we'll just wait until tomorrow afternoon when I'll pretend to get a call from my office about some stock-market emergency."

"Max," she pointed out, "there can't be any stock emergency on a Sunday—the market is closed."

"It'll be Monday in Australia," he replied, "and I'm an international sort of guy. Besides, I don't think Carlo's gonna argue about a chance to get you alone."

The very idea of that made Kimberly shiver inside, but she knew it was their goal. She also knew that she wouldn't *really* be alone with him—Max would secretly be in the closet. Besides, she reminded herself, she was tough and emotionless now, all business, and she intended to keep it that way until this assignment was over. She was ready to take Carlo on.

"So then," she replied, "after your imaginary call, I'll keep Carlo busy on the patio or something while you go get set up in the closet?"

He nodded. "Right. The camera equipment is already there, so it shouldn't take long. Give me five minutes or so and then you can come up. If Carlo doesn't suggest looking at your jewelry himself, you can offer to show it to him. And then we can bring this baby home."

"Sounds good," she said.

"Do you have any questions about your part?"

"I just act submissive and passionate and let Carlo do the rest, right?"

"Right."

"Then when things heat up a little, I act like I've changed my mind. I decline his advances and rush from the room, leaving him alone with the jewelry, right?"

"Right again."

"And if things get out of hand, you'll be there. Right?"

"Right a third time."

Kimberly nodded, then turned to leave the office, when Max said, "Oh, and...Brandt?"

She stopped and glanced back at him. "Yeah?"

"At dinner, you can, uh, hold off on the touchy-feely stuff. I think he's got the message that you don't mind him hanging around you."

Inside, Kimberly's stomach roiled with anger, but she was a professional—an *unemotional* professional— so on the outside she worked to remain very calm. "Yeah, I already picked up on your feelings about that."

She started to go then, but stopped and looked back once more. "By the way, Tate, the next time you hire a woman to play this kind of role, you might want to spell out your expectations a little more clearly. You know, one touch by the pool, not two, that sort of thing. It's kind of hard to play by your rules when I don't know them." She'd decided to be cool, but that didn't mean she couldn't make smart remarks.

She turned and walked out, then went down the hall

to the kitchen. She caught a glimpse of Carlo through the French doors, his back to them, so thankfully he hadn't seen her. She could use a few more minutes without the lout bothering her.

A minute later, Max caught up with her. "Looks like we've got a few minutes to kill," he said, "so I might as well make use of it."

"How?"

"I'm gonna go search Carlo's room."

Kimberly tilted her head. "And what do you expect to find? The guy's only been here since last night."

"Possibly nothing, but you never know. A phone number of a contact, a matchbook from someplace he hangs out, some kind of a clue to where the jewelry goes when it leaves the victims."

Kimberly shrugged. She doubted he'd turn up anything, but she supposed it was worth a try.

"Your job is to keep him from coming in and surprising me."

She grimaced. "I'm not crazy about being alone with the doofus, you know."

"You won't have to be. Just stay here and keep an eye on him from a distance. If he comes inside and you need me, just tell him you're hungry and yell up that you're ready to leave for dinner."

"All right," she said. Sounded easy enough.

Kimberly stationed herself at the table in the breakfast nook and Max headed upstairs. Staring out the window, she pondered Max's instructions for dinner—no more touching. That was more than fine with her, but she was slightly afraid it might confuse Carlo. What was Max's problem here, anyway? After all, if all he felt for her was lust, what difference did it make who touched her?

The French doors opened then, drawing her from her thoughts. She looked up to see Carlo and pasted on a smile. "Hi."

"Hi there." He walked up and gave her a thorough once-over, something she was beginning to think of as his trademark greeting. "You look great."

"Thanks." She gazed at him from beneath flirtatiously slanted lashes, then stood up. "Well, I don't know about you, but I'm starving. Shall I get Max and we can go to dinner?"

"You know, actually, I need to make a phone call first, if you don't mind. I'll just go upstairs and use the phone in my room." And to her great astonishment— after all, Carlo was not one to squander a moment alone with her—he began to head toward the stairs. Toward his room. Where Max was.

"Wait."

He stopped and looked back.

"Why don't you use the phone in Max's office down the hall? Save you the trip upstairs. Then I'll get Max and we'll be ready to go when you're done." She offered him a wide smile for good measure.

He returned the wide smile, but didn't go along with her suggestion. "That's okay. I need to get my shoes while I'm up there." Only then did she glance down and see that beneath his khaki trousers his feet were bare. Damn.

Kimberly quickly considered her options. She could yell for Max, but what could she say that would make sense at this point and not sound suspicious? She couldn't yell, "Let's go to dinner," because Carlo had just said he wasn't ready to leave yet. And she certainly couldn't shout, "Carlo's coming upstairs!" She knew she should be able to think faster than this, but her mind went blank. She couldn't come up with one plausible thing to say to get Max out of Carlo's room.

Then an idea hit her. It was fairly lame, but so was Carlo, so maybe it would be okay. "Carlo, would you be a dear and do me a favor first?" This time she even fluttered her eyelashes, feeling a little desperate.

The request, thankfully, seemed to abate his hurry. "For you, gorgeous, anything."

She giggled for him, having picked up on the fact that he liked the dumb-girlishness of the sound, and then shifted her attention to a philodendron in a brass planter situated on a high ledge in the kitchen. "I've been trying to figure out how I could get that plant down to repot it, but I just don't think I can reach it." For added effect, she added, "I've been asking Mrs. Leland to do it for weeks, but she keeps forgetting. And the poor plant needs some attention. So do you think you could get it down for me?"

"Hmm. Well, I can try...."

She understood Carlo's hesitation. The ledge was clearly too tall for him, as well. She wondered vaguely how anyone could get the plant down, or even water it. "I'll bet if you got up on the counter you might be able to reach it. Will you try for me?"

"Of course. Like I said, anything for you."

Carlo approached the kitchen counter and climbed up onto it. "You know," she said, "we have a footstool in one of the upstairs closets. I'll just run up and get it for you."

Then she scurried from the kitchen and up the stairs,

straight into Carlo's room. Max was bent over the desk going through Carlo's wallet. He looked up at her like a man who'd been caught stealing jewelry. "What are you doing? Trying to shave a few years off my life?"

She kept her voice low. "We've gotta get out of here. He's coming up. There's nothing I could do to prevent it."

Max took a step toward her, looking completely irritated. "How about yelling for me? Did we not have a plan?"

"It didn't seem prudent given the circumstances. Now, if you'll just quit arguing and—"

He took another step closer and clamped a hand over her mouth, silencing her. Then they both heard it—the faint but distinct sound of footsteps padding down the hall. "Damn it," he muttered beneath his breath.

They both knew it was too late to get out now.

Kimberly scanned the room. "The closet."

6

MAX MOVED BRISKLY toward the closet and opened the sliding door, stepping inside. Then he grabbed Kimberly's wrist and pulled her in with him, although it was close quarters and their bodies were crushed together. Apparently the house's owners used this closet for storage as it was crammed with boxes and garment bags. A murmured curse left him as he attempted to find a more comfortable position behind her. "Try turning around," he whispered, so she did, plastering her back against his chest. He slid the door shut just before they heard Carlo enter the room.

Max stood statue-still, waiting for something to happen. Two things promptly did. He heard Carlo pick up the phone and begin to dial. And he felt Kimberly shift her weight from one foot to the other, moving against him in the process.

He was getting hard. That quickly. He squeezed his eyes shut as his arousal pressed into her bottom through their clothing.

He wanted to bang his head against the wall. *Somebody put me out of my misery.* Why couldn't he stop this? He'd as much as blamed her earlier for their unprofessional behavior, but the fault was all his. His and his uncontrollable desire for her. How could he be getting an erection now, while they were hiding in the closet, while they were in direct danger of being discovered? This was not the time to lose control of himself again, and considering that their bodies were practically cemented together, there was nothing he could do to keep her from feeling it. Things were going quickly from bad to worse.

"This is Carlo," Max suddenly heard him say outside the closet. "Yeah, you should see this place, man— out of this world."

So someone else knew Carlo was here. That was a beginning, the start of a clue.

By all rights, Carlo's conversation should have taken Max's mind off his pants and fully onto his job, but that didn't appear to be happening. What was going on down there didn't exactly seem to be a matter of the mind. He grew harder against Kimberly's soft bottom and wondered if she felt it yet.

"They're loaded," Carlo said, and then he lowered his voice so that Max could barely make out the next part. "Haven't seen most of the goods yet, but the husband has been talking them up like they're the crown jewels. Ought to be a hell of a heist."

Okay, this was big. Whoever Carlo was talking to knew he was here to steal jewelry. *Keep talking, Carlo,* he willed silently. *Tell me what I need to know.* At the same time, Max was also thinking, *Get off the phone, Carlo, before one of us loses our balance and goes tumbling out the door. Before my preoccupation with my partner's body becomes any more obvious than it already must be.* He couldn't believe how much he wanted to touch her.

"They asked me to stay the weekend. Not sure if it'll stretch out any longer than that."

No, Max more than wanted to touch her. He wanted

to be inside her. He wanted to push up her skirt, pull down her panties and be inside her.

"Oh man, the wife is incredible." Carlo had lowered his voice again, but went on. "All curves and legs. And pretty friendly, too. I don't think I'll have much of a problem with her."

Oh yeah, you will, buddy. Lay another finger on her and you're a dead man.

But Carlo had one thing right. Was she ever incredible. At the moment, Max was wondering how he'd ever let her go in the first place—ruined career or no ruined career. Yet her beauty and her body were only two parts of the equation. She was smart. And she was funny. And she was passionate...oh God, was she passionate.

Max muttered a silent oath. Kimberly's passion was definitely the wrong thing to be thinking about right now. But a flashback—her on top of him on a rainy Sunday morning three years ago, making love to him until they were both weak—increased Max's longing for her. He knew she felt his arousal now—it would be impossible for her not to.

All he could do was hold still against her and wait for Carlo to get off the phone and leave.

He wanted her even more now than he had a minute ago, if that was possible.

"Don't worry, boss," Carlo was saying, catching Max's attention again. The whole phone call was finally proof that he wasn't working alone, but this last part meant he wasn't even the guy in charge. "I've got it all under control. You'll have the stuff before you know it."

He put his hand on Kimberly's shoulder, his way of

saying silently, *Did you hear that?* But in the meantime he was touching her someplace else, too—this one not quite as innocent. Big news or not, he decided that as soon as Carlo left the room, he wanted to yank Kimberly down on the floor of the closet, let their limbs and bodies get completely entwined, and then make hot, slow love to her until she screamed. Not that he could do any of that. But it was the thought that invaded his brain. *Come on, Carlo, get off the phone before I lose my remaining control, little as it may be.*

Kimberly took a deep breath and tried not to move. The slightest flinch or waver and she would feel him that much more, pressing into the cleft of her bottom. And she would want him that much more.

She wanted to stomp her feet in frustration. She wasn't going to feel this! She just wasn't!

But she did.

It didn't matter what she'd told herself just a little while ago about being a professional. And it didn't matter how angry Max made her with his irrational reactions. To Kimberly, it had been an eternity since he had touched her by the pool today. She hadn't known it, hadn't let herself recognize her own hunger, but now she needed him. She needed his touch, needed his body pressing up against hers.

Currently she *had* the second part.

Even as she knew how badly she desired it, it was killing her inside.

She wanted to cry at the way she ached for him. It wasn't fair! When would this job be over? When would she get Max Tate out of her system once and for all?

Then an overwhelming sadness hit her, amid her wild longing for him. She would probably *never* get

Max out of her system. If three years hadn't been enough to do it, how many years would? She had a very scary feeling that she was going to be in love with him for the rest of her life and that there wasn't a damn thing she could do about it.

Oh God, she thought desperately. And she wanted to lean back against him even closer, wanted to be wrapped in his arms, just wanted him to hold her and let her savor these strange moments in case they were the last physical connection with him she would ever feel.

"All right then," she heard Carlo say into the phone. "See you after I get what I came for." Concluding with a soft laugh, he hung up.

Kimberly bit her lip, still thinking far more about being pressed against Max than listening to Carlo. *Oh, Max, Max, sweet, sexy Max.* Well, she amended, he *could* be sweet when he wasn't being resentful. And he was *always* sexy. She sighed and again chided herself for the terrible mistake she'd made that day three years ago with Margaret Carpenter.

Outside the closet, she heard Carlo moving around, putting his shoes on, she guessed. A moment later, everything went quiet and she knew he was gone.

Inside, she and Max remained still, and Kimberly closed her eyes, bit her lip and did what she'd done before—savored the moment, the connection with this man she loved, this man who lusted for her, this man who could never love her back because he thought she'd betrayed him.

Finally, he whispered, "Well, I guess you'd better, uh, open the door now."

"Right," she replied, and then she slid the door to

the left, admitting the daylight from the room's window and ending the strange, forced intimacy they'd just shared.

Stepping away from him and out of the closet was more difficult than she'd imagined. It left her feeling oddly empty, oddly alone. Still, she wasted no time in moving toward the door, tossing over her shoulder in a voice far too breathy for her liking, "I'm gonna go freshen up a bit. I'll meet you downstairs."

"Kimberly, wait."

The request made her catch her breath. She turned to face him and gathered the courage to cautiously meet his eyes.

"I'm...sorry about that. In the closet."

Oh God. She really didn't want to talk about... She couldn't...*wouldn't*. "Sorry about what?" She shook her head lightly and feigned ignorance.

He blinked. "You know. About..."

She shook her head again. "No, I don't know. What?"

Max sighed and now it was his turn to give his head a vague sort of shake. "Nothing. Never mind."

"All right. I'll meet you downstairs in a minute."

And then she was out of the room and in their suite and in the bathroom, holding on to the counter and thinking, *How much longer can I do this?*

A FEW MINUTES LATER, Kimberly hooked up with Max at the bottom of the stairs. "Where is he?" she whispered.

"Back out by the pool," Max replied with a roll of his eyes in Carlo's general direction. "He *loves* that thing."

Kimberly nodded and suddenly remembered Max

pressing against her in the closet. Part of her wanted to leap on him and part of her still wanted to cry. She prayed neither desire showed on her face.

"How about that phone call?" Max said then, smiling. A real smile, Kimberly thought, honest and happy and without even a hint of malice. She loved that smile, and she had missed it, apparently more than she'd realized, because it warmed her heart nearly to bursting.

"Pretty insightful," she managed to choke out.

"So Carlo's just a middleman," Max mused. "Possibly even the low man in the operation."

"Sounded that way to me," she agreed.

"This explains why he was never caught with any evidence." He continued to smile and Kimberly smiled back at Max's sudden exuberance over this discovery, trying to be happy for him, happy for them both that they were making a little headway and finding out something the police had been unable to discover. But it was hard, considering all the horrible heartbreak and frustration she still suffered on the inside.

BY THE TIME they actually left for dinner with Carlo, Kimberly managed to feel a little better, a little more confident. She had to, after all. She had to be in character, and she wanted to play her part perfectly to pull this off for Max. Not just to show him she was a good P.I. but also because it was nice to see him happy.

It was only when they reached the Porsche that they realized they had a problem—it was a two-seater. "Hmm, this won't work, will it?" Max murmured. Kimberly knew he was trying to hide the troubled expression that wanted to reveal itself.

"How about taking the Jag?" Carlo suggested. The

Jaguar. The one he'd seen in the garage. The one that not only didn't belong to them, but which they also didn't have keys for.

"Uh, well..." Max stammered.

Kimberly rescued him with what she hoped wasn't too lame of an answer. "That's cute, honey, but you don't have to be embarrassed to tell Carlo the truth about the cars."

Max looked at her, his eyes half alight with hope, but also with the question, Where are you going with this?

"The thing is," she said, turning to Carlo, "Max babies those cars to death. Only takes them out once or twice a year, and that's when we've checked the weather report to make sure there isn't a drop of rain in sight. Even then he won't park them in a parking lot where there are other cars—too afraid of getting a ding in the door. They're his hobby. Aren't they, Max?"

"Um, yeah." He nodded.

"You should see him, out here waxing them, polishing the dashboards. I think he dotes on them more than I do on my diamonds."

Good girl, Kimberly, Max thought, relief flowing through him.

"So you wouldn't mind driving us to dinner, would you, Carlo?" he asked. He even stepped up to slap Carlo on the back.

"Well, I'd love a ride in the Jag, but...what the hell." He smiled. "Hop in."

The ride to the bistro in Carlo's late-model Camaro was fairly uneventful except that Max cringed each time Carlo shifted gears because his hand got so close to Kimberly's perfect knees. She rode in the front, of course, and Max sat in the back. He kept a close eye on those knees, whose perfection he'd never really noticed so much before right now.

Getting out of the car, Max decided to deter any touchy-feely plans Carlo might have for his "wife" by taking her hand on the way into the restaurant. She peered up at him, a flicker of surprise flashing through her eyes, but he gave her a quick wink and a knowing look and hoped she understood that he was just doing his part to keep Carlo's hands off her.

The bistro had a quaint outdoor-seating area that edged a wooded hillside. The trio was shown to an umbrella-covered table near the white picket fence that enclosed the area, and Max couldn't help thinking that it would make for a pleasant evening if Carlo hadn't been here. His hunger for Kimberly in the closet hadn't exactly faded over the half hour since it had happened, and he could imagine having a quiet dinner with her as dusk fell to night around them, their passion escalating with the decreased light. He'd reach out to touch her, first his hand on hers, then his fingers would glide sensually up her arm in a whispery caress. They would read the need in each other's eyes and he'd say to her very softly, "Let's get out of here." The ride to his place or to hers would be silent, but sexually charged, and then he'd slowly strip that pretty little dress off her and he'd get thoroughly reacquainted with her body. They wouldn't stop until the sun came up tomorrow morning.

"Max?"

Her voice jolted him from the fantasy and he looked up to see that the waitress stood poised to write down his drink order. "Uh, bring me a beer. Whatever you have on tap." The waitress nodded quickly and went on her way. Max realized immediately he'd stepped out of character—stockbroker Max Tate would have ordered wine or at the very least, an imported beer. But Carlo, as usual, was too busy mooning over Kimberly to notice and Max felt thankful he hadn't slipped up on anything more important than that. *Get a hold of yourself, Tate, before you screw this thing up.*

Whatever was going on in his head for Kimberly was trouble, plain and simple. When he looked up to catch her smiling, it actually felt like more than lust, because he felt it in his gut as much as in his pants. Lust was usually a very straightforward and simple thing for him, a pants-only experience.

But, he reasoned, he and Kimberly had a history. Kind of a big one. So, of course, lusting for her would be more complicated. He shook his head. This was not what he needed. No way. *One more day, pal,* he lectured himself. *Hang on for one more day and then you can go home and be done with this stupid charade.*

After their drinks arrived and they ordered dinner, Max turned his thoughts, and the conversation, to something that might be useful. He tried to casually wheedle out of Carlo anything about who else he knew in the city, who his friends were, what he did in his free time, but the guy wouldn't give an inch. He claimed he'd just moved here a few months ago and didn't know anybody. "That's why it's such a pleasure to meet you both," he said. "I mean, I really appreciate you taking the time to educate me about the stock market, Max. But more than that, I appreciate how you've opened your home to me this weekend, as well as given me the opportunity to get to know Kimberly." And then, of course, he grinned lasciviously at her, because he couldn't seem to be in her presence for more than a few seconds without doing that, the slimeball.

Kimberly tilted her head and returned the smile and Max's stomach tightened.

Then Carlo leaned toward her. "Oops. You have a little speck of something right..." he lifted a fingertip to the corner of her mouth "...here."

Kimberly giggled and it all served to make Max go even crazier inside. He wanted to fly across the table and rip Carlo's arm from its socket. He knew it was simply some combination of his ego combined with his desire, but he just couldn't control how crazy it made him.

Instead of flying across the table, though, Max opted for a much calmer and more effective reaction. He, too, leaned forward and deftly slid his hand to Kimberly's face, gently turning her toward him.

Her eyes widened on him prettily, looking tonight as rich and green as the foliage beyond the fence, and he liked what he saw in her gaze. Despite all the ups and downs of the day, he could tell she still wanted him, just as she had by the pool. "What?" she whispered.

"Just checking to make sure Carlo got whatever it was." He'd spoken throatily, not by design but because that's just how his voice came out when he was touching her.

"Don't worry," Carlo said. "I got it."

But for Max, Carlo wasn't even there anymore. There was only her perfect mouth, half-open and looking delectable, and her perfect eyes, all wide and wanting.

He leaned forward to kiss her, slow, gentle, short, chaste...and electrifying. He pulled back and saw the weakness in her eyes and it sent a bolt of longing to his pants, arousing him all over again. Oh damn. How would he possibly stand this for another whole day?

ALONE IN THE MASTER SUITE Kimberly felt as if she'd been run over by a truck. This had been the longest day of her life. At least on the day when she'd lost her job and Max at the same time, it had happened all at once, quickly, but this...*this* was a nightmare. Between Carlo's unwanted touches and Max's scintillating ones, her poor body didn't know *what* to feel. It was hard going from repulsion to passion and back again, over and over and over.

She bit her lip, remembering Max's kiss at dinner. What on earth had that been about? Was he trying to save her from Carlo or trying to remind her that he thought she'd gone too far physically with their suspect? Or was it just more lust? *That, Kimberly, was lust.* The words from earlier rang in her head. They still hurt to remember. And yet, maybe it was better than nothing. Even if he didn't love her, she couldn't deny that it excited her to know he still desired her.

She sat on the bed playing with the faux diamonds from the safe. This was the first chance she'd had to familiarize herself with the jewelry, as Max had told her to when they'd first arrived. She'd left the two men sitting by the pool with glasses of wine a few minutes ago—dinner had yielded no new information on Carlo, but Max was still working at it. Kimberly, however, was more than ready to be off-duty, thankful for a precious bit of privacy.

She pulled extravagant necklaces and bracelets from the round box, enamored of their exquisite beauty—

fakes or not—but really too tired to concentrate on what she was doing. Still, she examined them and practiced working the clasps, admittedly a good idea on Max's part because some of them were unusual and took a little time to operate efficiently.

"Ouch," she groaned. Then she dropped the necklace in her hands to the pile that now streamed from the jewelry box onto the brocade comforter. She was the only person she knew who could actually pinch her finger in a necklace clasp. She decided to take a break, get ready for bed, then look at the baubles a little more before returning them to the safe.

Standing up, Kimberly moved to the light switch on the wall to dim the lamps. Even her eyes were tired, and besides, a full moon shone through the balcony doors to gently illuminate the room.

She reached behind her to unzip her dress, then let it drop to her ankles. Stepping free of it, and of her shoes, she put them away in the closet. She was well ready to retire for the night—God knew she needed some serious sleep to recover from this day and get her wits about her for tomorrow—but first she needed to figure out what to wear to bed. As she'd decided earlier, no way would she be caught dead in any of her little nighties. Considering all that had happened, Max would surely think she was trying to seduce him and she definitely didn't want that.

For one thing, she didn't want to give him that kind of satisfaction. Her physical responses to him so far were bad enough. Considering how their relationship had ended so abruptly, she didn't want him to think she missed him or needed him as much as she still did.

And for another, she wasn't sure she could take having sex with him. Oh sure, she could *take* it. She'd *love* to take it. But afterward, she didn't know how she'd cope. Even as she longed for it with every ounce of her being, she also knew it would be disastrous for her. She couldn't go through that again, have that ultimate connection with him, only to say goodbye tomorrow when this was all over.

A knock came on the door. Oh drat, she wasn't ready yet. In fact, a quick look through her stuff confirmed what she already knew—she had nothing suitable to wear. Then it hit her! Maybe she'd snoop through the stuff in the closet that wasn't hers and find some nice full-length pajamas. She'd wash and return them after and no one would be the wiser.

Well, no time for searching out pajamas now. She was standing there in a pink lace bra and panties, and Max was at the door. He knocked again, impatiently this time.

"Just a minute," she yelled. She took a quick scan of the closet until she located a short, shiny, gold kimono hanging on a hook behind the door. She snatched it up and slid it on, quickly cinching the tie in front. After all, if she was going to borrow things from the lady who lived here, why not start now?

She padded quickly to the door and opened it.

And Carlo stepped in.

Kimberly's heart went wild. She tried to smile, but feared it had come out looking more like the complete shock that currently assaulted her. Why hadn't she asked who it was first?

But it was too late to lament a mistake. She had to stay sharp, no matter how tired or unprepared she was for this.

"Hi there." He wore a big, goofy smile.

"Hi."

"Hope I didn't catch you at a bad time, but—"

"Actually, you did."

"I was hoping I could entice you into a nightcap."

Where's Max? she wanted to ask, but she didn't want Carlo to think she was afraid. Still, this was not the plan. Not the plan at all.

"You know, Carlo, I'm really tired. If you don't mind, I'd rather just turn in. But I'll see you tomorrow—"

"Wow," he said then, ignoring her.

Kimberly followed his eyes to the jewelry that still lay strewn across the bed. Apparently, this was the one thing Carlo liked gaping at more than her, but even that didn't last for long. He quickly shifted his hungry gaze from the jewels to Kimberly's face, and then down to the silk kimono she wore. He gave her a flirtatious grin. "This is like kismet. Did you know I was coming?" He casually pushed the door so that it was almost shut.

Kimberly swallowed. This was bad. Really bad. Not only did he think she had the jewelry out because she wanted to show it to him, but he also thought she was wearing a tiny little robe because she wanted to show *herself* to him. She supposed it was no wonder after her performance over the last twenty-four hours, but still, this wasn't how things were supposed to go!

"Have you seen Max?" she asked.

He shook his head with a lecherous smile. "Don't worry about Max. It's just you and me."

Oh God, that was the truth. It was just the two of them, no Max, no protection.

But she could handle it. She *would* handle it. She was a trained professional and she could ease her way through this and come out all right. More teasing, she decided. She would simply consider this more teasing for the big oaf. She'd show him the jewelry, then insist on putting it away. She would promise to give him a closer, longer look at it tomorrow and imply that it would also include a closer, longer look at her, too. Kimberly hated to play it this way, but she didn't see that she had any other choice at the moment. To totally refuse his advances might make him hesitate tomorrow when they wanted him to steal the jewelry.

"Put it on for me," he said.

She lifted her gaze to him. Hid her nervous swallow. Smiled. "Put...what on for you?"

"Your jewelry. I want to see it on you."

"Carlo, this is really quite silly." She'd decided on a small attempt to dissuade him, but added a giggle just to keep him happy.

He stepped forward, closer to her. "Silly? For me to want to see these beautiful jewels gracing your neck, your wrist? Come on, Kimberly. Humor me."

She took a step back, toward the bed, toward the jewels. She still didn't like doing this—not at all—but if she appeased him a bit, it would be easier to get him to leave, easier to promise there would be more tomorrow. Tomorrow, when Max would be in the closet and everything would be how it was supposed to be.

She slid a flamboyant three-tiered diamond choker from the velvet box, then immediately realized she couldn't work the clasp and put it on herself without the aid of a mirror. Still, she attempted it anyway, opening the clasp, then putting the choker around her neck and trying to fasten it without seeing. She failed. Carlo immediately said, "Let me help you."

He stepped up and fastened the choker behind her neck while she held up her hair. When he stepped away, she breathed a huge sigh of relief that he hadn't taken the opportunity to start touching her.

"But wait," he said as she turned to face him. "The bracelet, too."

Oh brother, he'd noticed the matching bracelet lying on the bed. Kimberly sighed and reached for it, thankfully able to put this one on herself. Then she turned toward him again, and stood there letting him look at her, feeling horribly on display and horribly worried about this whole situation. Where in the world was Max?

"Beautiful," Carlo said of the jewels. "Exquisite."

She tried to smile, but it was getting harder all the time. Dear God, she wore only this little robe over her underwear, which could fall open at any time. Then what? Well, she decided, desperate times called for desperate measures.

"I'm glad you like it, Carlo," she said, "and I'll tell you a secret. If you come back tomorrow, I'll put it *all* on for you. And I won't be wearing this silly robe with it, either. How would you like that?"

His eyes brightened. "I'd like that a lot."

"Good." Her smile was sincere this time, because it appeared he was going to leave peacefully.

Then across the room, the door opened...and Max came in.

Kimberly saw his eyes blaze instantly. "What the hell's going on here?"

Carlo turned to face him, his eyes wide, his complexion suddenly ashen. "This isn't like it seems, Max buddy. Honest."

Max took a menacing step forward. "How is it, then?"

"I was just, uh, taking a look at Kimberly's jewelry. Those pieces in particular fascinated me and I couldn't truly see how they looked without her putting them on."

"And as for why my wife is standing there in her robe?"

Kimberly took this one, at the same time trying to save her own skin. "Carlo knocked on the door while I was changing clothes, honey. Nothing to be alarmed about."

"Nothing to be alarmed about," Max repeated evenly, shifting his gaze from Kimberly to Carlo. "Is that true, Carlo?"

"Of course, Max. Of course. Nothing happened, nothing at all. I would never betray your hospitality that way. You've been so good to me, taken me into your home, given me your friendship, and I would never try to—to…"

Carlo finally gave up on finishing his pleas and Max stood looking back and forth between them, as if he was mulling it all over. Finally he took a deep breath. "All right then."

"Really?" Carlo asked. "It's all right?"

"Well, I don't think it's a good idea that you're in our bedroom, but—"

"You're right, of course it's not. I was just inviting Kimberly to join us for a drink, but don't worry, it won't happen again."

"Good enough," Max said.

"So, me and you, we're cool?" Carlo asked, eyebrows lifting.

Slowly, Max nodded. "But I think it's time for Kimberly and me to retire, so good night."

Carlo hurried to the door. "Good night. And I'm sorry to have caused any...*confusion.*"

They both waited until the door closed and then Max turned to face her. She was so lovely. The diamonds shimmered at her throat. The silk robe she wore was open slightly, just enough to reveal a shadowy bit of cleavage.

But at the moment, how good she looked was completely secondary to his anger.

"What were you doing? Are you crazy?" He kept his voice to a heated whisper. "We had a plan, a specific plan, and we had it for a reason, Brandt. Can't I depend on you to do anything right?" Yes, it was a direct jab regarding the Carpenter case, but he didn't care—he was too mad to care right now—even when he saw the rage flare in her eyes.

"For your information, I didn't go against your precious plan," she said, keeping her voice low, as well. "He just came in. I was changing clothes, there was a knock on the door, and I threw on this robe. I answered, expecting it to be you."

"So when it turned out to be him you just thought, 'Let's have a practice run,' and yanked open the safe for him?"

"No! Before he arrived, I was practicing with the jewelry like you told me. He saw it and asked me to put it on. What was I supposed to do?"

"Tell him some other time. Like when I can be in the closet, damn it."

"It wasn't that easy, Tate."

"What if he'd taken the jewelry? What if he'd gotten away with it without us getting it on video?" Max went silent at the strange sensation that grew in his chest with his next thought. It felt as though his heart was bending, breaking. "What if...he'd forced you...without me here to stop him?"

He lifted his gaze, surprised to see how truly upset she looked. She muttered her answer. "What do you care, anyway?"

Max took a deep breath. He didn't think anyone had ever said anything so insulting to him in his life. "You might think I'm a Class A jerk, Brandt, but I'm not *that* bad a guy. You may have ruined my entire career once upon a time, but I don't hate you. You and I, we...well, you should know me well enough to know I wouldn't want anything to happen to you." He'd said more than he'd wanted, but still hadn't told her the way he really felt. At this moment, he thought he'd die if anything bad ever happened to her. Even though it wasn't his fault, he still wished he had been there, wished he'd been more aware of where she and Carlo had been, of where he himself should have been.

Then he saw one shiny tear rolling down her cheek in the moonlit room. The diamonds and the teardrop shimmered in startling contrast against her silken skin. He hated that he'd made her cry. Hated it.

"That's always what it comes back to, isn't it?" she said in a voice so soft he barely recognized it. "Our history. Our past. What I did to you. You can't find a way to look beyond it. You can't even *try* to forgive me."

"Kimberly," he whispered, taking a step closer to her, closing the gap between them. "You have to understand how I felt then. I had worked my whole life to get where I was. That job was everything to me. To have the rug pulled out from under me like that, to lose it all in under two minutes flat... I was devastated."

"That's how you felt *then*," she said. "But how do you feel *now*?"

That was a good question. One Max didn't know the answer to. So he didn't reply. He simply stepped close to her, because the one thing he did know was that this was where he wanted to be. And he realized that her robe had come untied and fallen open and whatever she wore underneath was scant and lacy and pale. He met her gaze, her eyes soft and without distinct color in the dimly lit room.

"Look how beautiful you are like this."

Her voice was barely audible. "What?"

"All dripping and shimmering with diamonds and tears. I'm sorry, Kimberly, sorry to make you cry." Then he attempted a gentle smile. "They look good on you." He felt the need to add, "The diamonds. Not the tears."

"They're fake," she reminded him. "The diamonds. Not the tears."

"They're still beautiful. Particularly beautiful on you, babe. What man could resist you?"

"You do pretty well," she muttered.

He immediately shook his head, unable to believe she really thought that. "Not so well," he told her. "Have you already forgotten what happened by the pool?"

He watched as she bit her lip. If she had forgotten, she was clearly remembering it now. He reached up to wipe her solitary tear away with the back of his thumb.

He didn't want to see anything on her face but the desire he knew she felt for him.

Then he lowered his hand to her hip inside the robe, his fingertips meeting with soft lace, his palm with her flesh. A mix of sensations sent his need rocketing out of control. Slowly, he slid his hand up her body, stopping it next to her breast. "Did it feel good today by the pool, Kimberly? Me touching you."

"Yes," she whispered.

"Does this feel good?" He reached out his thumb to stroke her nipple through the lace of her bra and felt it bead instantly beneath his touch.

"Yes." Her voice trembled.

Max knew he'd gone too far. And he also knew he was just about to go much further. He leaned close to her ear. "Let me do things to you, Kimberly. Let me take you to bed. Let me make love to you."

7

IT HAD SEEMED like an eternity for Kimberly between this morning at the pool and the closet this evening. Now it seemed like an eternity since the closet and this—Max's hand on her aching breast, and his raspy voice in her ear, whispering the hottest invitation she'd ever received.

She knew she should find the strength to say no because she knew, by his own admission, that all he felt for her was lust. But he'd made her so weak. Weak and hungry. It was a horrible, wonderful culmination of all the emotions and sensations she'd experienced since seeing him again. And she was too weak, too hungry to say no. If lust was all she could have from him, she'd take it.

"Oh, Max..." she breathed.

He was still near her ear—she could still feel his breath. "Say yes, Kimberly. Tell me you want me as much as I want you."

"Oh yes, Max, I want you. You know I do."

He let out a heavy sigh that struck Kimberly as rapturous relief. Then he was lowering warm, soft kisses to her neck and gently raking his teeth down her earlobe. She pulled in her breath at the incredible sensation of it, thinking, *We're really going to do this, we're really going to make love.* Suddenly she couldn't wait another minute, another second. She wanted him so much more than she ever had before, more than she'd even known was possible.

His kisses moved to her mouth—hot, delicate kisses that seemed to wrap around her and take hold of her soul. He cupped both of her breasts in his hands and she sighed again. How badly she had yearned for this. For three long, lonely years she had waited, dreamed, of being in Max's arms again.

She kissed him some more, kissed him as he kneaded her breasts, kissed him as he pushed the kimono off her shoulders and to the floor. He grazed one hand down over her hip, then let it dip teasingly between her legs before brushing his fingertips up over her bare stomach, finally stopping at the front clasp on her bra.

She felt the clasp come undone, the bra loosening around her. She loved the sensation of being undressed by him, even if she hadn't been wearing much in the first place. Pushing the lace cups aside, he rubbed his palms over her taut, sensitive nipples, gazing down at them. "You're so beautiful," he murmured.

He bent over her, raining tiny, fire-infused kisses to her nipples, flicking his tongue expertly over the hardened nubs until she thought he might drive her completely out of her mind. Then he took the tip of her breast into his mouth, hard and fervent, making her pant and whimper. "Oh, Max, it feels so good. Please don't stop. Please."

And then he stopped.

She wanted to kill him, but immediately remembered—Max's lovemaking was legendary. He knew exactly what to do and when to do it. Kimberly looked down into his eyes and he looked back, his gaze heated and knowing. She was at his mercy now and there was no taking control. She didn't even want to.

He kissed his way down her stomach and she tingled hotly below, waiting, waiting. And then came the sweet kisses on her thigh, edging upward with achingly slow precision until finally they met with her panties. He kneeled before her, gently moving the lace aside with rough fingertips, making Kimberly clench her fists and pull in her breath. Soon he began to kiss her there, pushing two fingers inside. She gasped, reaching over her head, clawing helplessly at the wall behind her so as not to collapse from the mind-crushing sensations. "Max." She didn't know if she was whispering or screaming at this point, and she didn't care.

He lifted one of her legs, placing her foot on a chair beside her, so he could reach her better. She clenched her teeth to keep from sobbing at how much she felt it, how his mouth was making her body shriek with ecstasy, how the sensations had now become wild pulses that rippled through her at lightning speed. It was about to happen, she knew, about to tear through her with all the power of a locomotive, about to bury her, and then...he was gone.

Rising, he took her in his arms, where she shivered and muttered, "Please, Max, why?"

"Shh." He soothed her, holding her close, dropping soft kisses on her neck, running his strong hands over the length of her back. "Don't worry, babe," he whispered. "We're not done yet. Not even close."

"But—" She'd been so on the edge, so deliciously

near, and he...he'd abandoned her. "Maybe *you* weren't close, but *I* was."

"Shh. Trust me." He began kissing her again, those same delicately passionate kisses that turned her inside out, and on second thought, this hardly felt like abandonment. *Trust me.* Oh yes, she did. She would.

Max pulled back from her and gently lowered her panties to her ankles to let her step free of them. He stood back, gazing on her nakedness, until finally he uttered, "You take my breath away, Kimberly."

He started undressing, too, unbuttoning his shirt and nearly ripping it off, yanking his shoes from his feet, pushing his blue jeans down and stepping out of them. Then he removed his briefs. She looked at him just as he'd looked at her—remembering, wanting. This was too much. "Don't make me wait, Max."

He shook his head and his voice came as breathy as hers. "I don't think I can."

He dug in his wallet for a condom and they fell frantically to the bed, both shoving the jewelry aside. He was inside her instantly. She was trying not to cry at how good it felt, at how much she loved him, at how right and perfect this seemed. He moved in her slow and deep and she felt it to her very core. Wrapping her legs around him, she never wanted to let him leave her, never wanted this glorious connection to end. *I love you, Max. Oh, how I love you.* She whispered the words to herself, over and over.

But then he pulled away from her yet again and she heard her own sob. She felt like a terribly impatient lover, but couldn't help how badly she needed him.

He rolled her onto her side and entered her from behind. She remembered telling him once that she could feel him deeper that way, and it was true, she still could. As she cried out with every thundering stroke, she knew she'd never felt this whole in her life—this right, this incredibly fulfilled. Having him inside her completed her in a way nothing else, no one else, ever could. It was a perfect moment in time, and she prayed it would never end.

He slid his hand over her hip and thigh, and began to gently stroke her with his finger. It was a sensation like velvet. She closed her eyes and just let herself feel it, let herself bask in it, until that glorious tension began to build inside her, began to fill her, driving her to move her body against his hand as he made love to her. And then it took her—the most startling release she'd ever known, stunning in its intensity, and beautiful because it was filled with all the love she felt for the man who had given it to her.

Soon he was coming, too, with a deep groan as he thrust hard inside her. Kimberly thought she would burst with emotion over the connection they shared, over the places they'd just taken each other.

They stayed quiet and still as he held her afterward, his arms wrapped around her from behind. She hoped he wouldn't notice her ridiculous reaction, but finally he leaned over and peered at her in the moonlight. "Are you crying?" he whispered.

She lifted a hand to wipe her tears away and tried to cover a necessary sniffle. "No."

"It's all right if you are, Kimberly," he murmured low and sweet. "It's okay." Then he lowered a gentle kiss to her cheek and lay back behind her, still holding her tight.

MAX LET the morning sun urge his eyes open. Looked like another beautiful day outside. A beautiful day to catch a thief, he thought. Then he glanced beside him in bed and saw Kimberly, bare but for the sheet that rose only to her waist, a diamond choker still circling her delicate neck. He closed his eyes again. She looked incredibly lovely. But he'd made a very big mistake.

He couldn't believe he'd let happen what he'd let happen. Well, maybe he could. It had seemed inevitable as the day had progressed yesterday, but it was completely unprofessional. Their lovemaking had stirred up some old feelings for her, tender feelings, but that didn't mean anything had changed.

The best thing he could do, he decided, would be to get out of bed, get in the shower, get dressed, get downstairs. Not make a big deal out of this. Move on.

He rolled over away from her, ready to push the covers back, when she stirred next to him.

He looked back at her. Watched her eyes flutter open. Watched her turn to him with a sleepy, sexy, sweet-as-candy smile. "Morning," she said, her voice butterfly soft.

As soon as Kimberly saw him, her thoughts—practically her whole being—leaped to last night. To the complete and utter fulfillment he'd given her, something that had felt far more than sexual, as if he'd somehow reached inside her and touched her soul.

"Uh, hi," he said, his gaze downcast. Only then did she really see him. The troubled expression shadowing his handsome face. The worry hanging over his dark eyes. His deep voice had sounded vaguely cool, dejected.

"Are you...okay?" she asked, praying, *Please, please*

don't do this, please don't act how I'm afraid you're going to act.

"Yeah, fine," he replied without looking at her. Then he reached over the side of the bed and grabbed his briefs. "We'd better get moving. Big day today."

She sighed, realizing he was going to act that way. As though nothing had happened. She couldn't stand that. In fact, she *wouldn't* stand for it.

She sat up in bed and stared at him. "Are you just going to pretend we didn't make love?"

Next to her, he sighed, but he still didn't look at her. "We shouldn't have. It's my fault. I'm sorry. I got too close to you and lost control."

Kimberly swallowed hard. He'd just made everything completely clear to her. Even after last night, all he felt for her was lust. Still. She knew she should have foreseen this and in fact, she had. She'd told herself over and over again that making love to Max would be a mistake because he would never return her feelings. She'd forgotten about that last part amid her ecstasy. Now it was slapping her in the face, hard. And it hurt just as much she'd imagined it would, maybe more, because imagined hurt was nothing like the real thing. Real hurt cut to the quick and you couldn't dull it and you couldn't escape it. It was just a part of you. Already, it felt like the biggest part of Kimberly.

"I have a suggestion, Tate," she said, not looking at him. "If Carlo's not around, stay away from me. That way you won't be tempted to lose control again." Then she got up and walked to the bathroom, slamming the door shut behind her.

MAX LOOKED after her, immediately missing the sight of her when she slammed the door. Apparently he'd handled this the wrong way. He hadn't meant to make her mad, he'd just thought it would be easier if they both got on with the business of doing this job.

He climbed out of bed and did his best to make it, fluffing the pillows and pulling the comforter up over it. Then he gathered the fake jewelry strewn around the bed and on the floor and put it all neatly back into the black velvet box, which he also found on the carpet at the foot of the bed.

Of course, when he thought about it, she was right—he could try to pretend this hadn't happened, but it had. And he didn't think he'd be forgetting about it anytime soon. He could still feel her creamy breasts filling his hands, and the way her body had opened so warm and moist to take him inside. He could still feel the way his heart had seemed to contract when she held him tight, when her breath sounded so ragged in his ear, and when she came—*especially* when she came. Talk about evoking emotions, he'd felt things he didn't even know names for.

Then she'd cried. He'd almost forgotten that part. She'd cried and he'd held her and he'd told her it was okay. He didn't even know what he'd meant by that.

Or maybe he did. Maybe he'd been saying, *It's okay to feel so much, because I feel it, too.*

Damn. It was true. He'd felt it, too.

He shook his head at the disarming realization, then grabbed his clothes and went to use the shower down the hall.

KIMBERLY STOOD in the shower letting the water cascade over her, hoping it would somehow wash away her mortification. But she knew water couldn't do that. Nor could tears. She'd been having so many inane wishes lately, ever since Max Tate had re-entered her life.

The very thought of him brought back memories of her humiliation. How she had begged him. How she had whimpered and sobbed and panted and pleaded and... He certainly wasn't the only one who'd lost control. Only her loss had been much more complete than his—she'd lost control of her body...and her heart.

She'd been so overcome with love for him that she'd cried afterward. How utterly embarrassing. Especially now that she knew it meant nothing to him, nothing at all.

Toweling off with one of the plush bath sheets from the enormous linen closet, she promptly dropped it in the laundry chute and stood before the pink marble sinktop to put on her moisturizer. Plush bath sheets, marble sinktops, suddenly none of the lavishness of their accommodations held the same awe for her that it had only a day or two ago. The fact was, it just wasn't important compared to her feelings, compared to her heart.

After moisturizing, she threw on denim shorts and a T-shirt—who cared if Carlo thought it was sexy or not?—then scooped up the choker and bracelet she'd set on the sink and came out into the bedroom.

She'd heard the door close a long time ago and knew Max wasn't there, but she was surprised to see that he'd made the bed and cleaned up the jewelry. He'd left the black velvet box sitting neatly on the bed, lid open, waiting for her to drop the missing items back inside.

She lay the gems back among the others, gently closed the box, then returned it to the safe. Kimberly felt a distinct sadness fall over her, because packing up the jewelry and closing it away seemed somehow like packing up her and Max's lovemaking and hiding it away, as well, which was obviously just what he wanted.

That made sense, she thought cynically, because the jewelry and the lovemaking had something else in common, too. Both were fake.

Come on, Brandt, she told herself. *Toughen up, you've got a job to do. You can cry your heart out later, but for now, it's back to work.* And with that, she went downstairs ready to put in this last day's work before calling it a day with him—forever.

MAX WASN'T much of a cook, but he'd found some heat-and-serve sausage in the freezer and a bunch of eggs, which he planned to scramble. He dug out a big bowl from an overhead cabinet and began breaking the eggs into it. He tried his hardest not to let himself remember similar breakfasts on mornings after making love to Kimberly. After all, this was much different. He would be setting three plates.

So now he'd admitted it to himself, he thought as he broke the eggs, one by one into some milk, throwing the white shells into a garbage can. He'd admitted that he felt something for her. Something big. Something jam-packed with emotion.

He wasn't ready for that because there was a lot to take into consideration here. For one thing, the job. For another, the Carpenter case and all the loss that had come with it.

He turned the heat on under the skillet, then held his hand over it until he felt his palm warming. Kimberly had been right, he'd never really thought about forgiving her for the Carpenter case. But not because he was a rotten hardhead of a guy. It was because she'd never been around for him to forgive. She'd walked out of the room, and he'd gone to Vegas and spent the next two and a half years rebuilding his business. Forgiveness had never been an issue.

He mixed the eggs and milk with a fork, an array of questions wandering through his head. Could he forgive her? Could he forget? Where did trust come into play here? Did he really believe he could trust her now? In business? In pleasure? That was the part that had been so hard to take. Being betrayed by your partner was one thing, but being betrayed by your lover was much worse.

In one way, he felt as if he didn't know her at all anymore—she was so much tougher and saucier now than she'd been then. But in another way, he felt as if he knew her completely. And as if he wanted to know her even more. If only he could forget...and forgive. She'd tried to explain her actions to him the other day and he'd refused to listen. Too afraid that whatever she said would never be enough. Too afraid to feel such betrayal and emptiness all over again.

He dumped the egg mixture into the hot frying pan, surprised by his thoughts. Did he really want to know her even more? If anyone had asked him three days ago, he'd have easily said no. But now things had changed. He'd spent some time with her, both as his pretend wife and also as Kimberly, the woman who had been his partner and his lover. It hit him suddenly that she was both of those things again, even if not by design. And as to whether he really wanted to know her more...well, his answer was a firm *maybe*. Again, it all came back to forgiving and forgetting, two things he didn't know if he was capable of doing.

But first things first, he thought adamantly, turning the eggs with a fork. He had to put Carlo and his boss or bosses behind bars and get his client's property back. Until that was over, he couldn't think about Kimberly.

He used the same fork to flip the sausages in another skillet, then shoved some bread into the toaster and got out three juice glasses. Then he looked up to see Kimberly walk in, wearing cutoffs and a T-shirt. He wanted to smile, but he didn't because he couldn't think about relationship possibilities right now and he didn't want her to be thinking about them either.

"Hope I'm not too dressed down," she said.

He gave his head a short shake. "No, I think we've already got him where we want him. You look fine. Nice." In fact, she looked like the old Kimberly he remembered. That rainy-day Kimberly. The easygoing girl he'd loved to be with, laugh with, watch TV with, do anything with. Make love to. He couldn't think of Kimberly back then without thinking about making love to her. They'd spent a lot of time in bed. Which probably explained why last night had felt so much like...coming home.

Damn it, he thought, shaking his head. Hadn't he just told himself he couldn't think about that anymore right now?

"What?" she said in response to his expression.

"Nothing." He looked away. "Can you, um, pour

the juice for me?" Then he started turning the eggs again, amazed that he hadn't scorched them by neglecting them for so long.

"Sure," she said.

"Any sign of him up there?" he asked as she pulled a glass container of orange juice from the fridge, looking very cute in her shorts.

"I heard the hall shower."

"Good," he said, although this was no time to be thinking about Kimberly's shorts—he needed to concentrate on business. "I'll plan on getting my imaginary call from the office around two. Are you ready for this?" He met her eyes for that last part. It was necessary to see how she reacted.

"More than." She sounded eager. Looked eager. Which was a good attitude for a P.I. Still, it suddenly bothered him. He tried to hide his dismay.

"What's wrong?" she asked anyway.

"Nothing." He turned his back on her, removing the scrambled eggs from the burner. To his unequaled surprise, he realized that he was having second thoughts about sending her in with Carlo. He couldn't believe he'd be willing to scrap this whole setup, but suddenly he was.

"Brandt, this might be too dangerous." He didn't look at her, instead spooning the fluffy eggs into a clear glass dish.

"Dangerous?" But even keeping his gaze down, he could almost see the way her eyes widened in shock.

"What if you can't hold him at bay?" he asked her. "What if he gets rough?"

"I can handle it. And you'll be right in the closet, remember?"

He sighed and shook his head. "Still, I don't know. I'm not sure I like it."

"You liked it fine before."

"That was then."

"Something change?"

It was as if she was daring him. To admit the sex had been more than sex, more than what he'd wanted or expected it to be. To admit that he worried for her, that he wanted to take care of her, protect her. As he'd just acknowledged, he wasn't ready to go there yet. "No," he finally said.

"Then come on, Tate, toughen up. This isn't that big of a deal."

He looked at her and she looked back. They gazed at each other for a long, painfully slow moment, and Max thanked God that she'd never been able to read his expression, or she'd see that he was having more of those damn tender emotions toward her again. No matter how he tried, he was having a hard time pushing them into the background where they belonged.

"What smells so good?" Max flinched and looked up. Carlo stood in the doorway. Thankfully it appeared that he missed the look they'd been sharing.

"Eggs," Max replied.

"And sausage," Kimberly said.

"Sounds great. I'm starving."

"Take a seat at the table," Max told the crook. "You, too, babe," he said to Kimberly. "I'll handle all this."

"So what's up for today?" Carlo asked as he sat down.

"Nothing special. Have anything in mind?" Max asked.

"I could go for some more time by the pool."

That Carlo, he was a sucker for that particular luxury. Thank goodness this house came with one; it had made the lunkhead easy to entertain. "Sounds good to me," Max said. "You, babe?"

Their eyes met. He could see her slipping into character as she gave him a smile. "You know how I love to soak in the sun. Sounds wonderful." Then she shifted her smile to Carlo, which Max hated. But he had to admit...she was good.

"HEY, KIMBERLY, watch this!"

Kimberly politely lifted her head from the lounge chair in time to see Carlo do a huge cannonball into the pool. How mature, she thought with a yawn. She waited for him to surface and said, "That was a good one, Carlo."

"Something to drink from inside, babe?" Max asked from his seat at one of the teak patio tables.

Babe. She was trying not to let the old endearment make her feel anything, but it still did. Especially now, after last night. "A wine cooler would be nice," she said.

She'd been trying desperately to come to grips with what Max's actions had made clear—he simply felt nothing for her beyond a sexual attraction. *Quit smiling at me with those seductive brown eyes,* she wanted to snap at him. *And quit calling me babe.* Because none of that was helping her keep her hold on the reality of this situation. Yet she knew it was necessary. For the rest of the day they were husband and wife, whether or not the pretense broke her heart more with each passing second.

"Here you go, babe."

She opened her eyes to find Max holding out a festive glass covered with bright tropical fish, the wine cooler poured thoughtfully over ice. He was smiling again. Damn him.

"Thanks." She reached up to take the glass with an obligatory smile that killed her, because inside she wanted to cry. She might be completely capable of nailing Carlo to the wall, but that didn't mean she still wasn't suffering the girlish emotions of unrequited love.

Kimberly's dainty fingers touched Max's as he passed her the drink and something inside him tingled as he pulled his hand away. He gave his head a short shake to shrug off the feeling and hoped she hadn't noticed, hoped she didn't start wondering just what was going on with him. Of course, he wondered that, too. This was getting worse, this situation with her.

To allay the feeling, he swung his gaze to where Carlo now sat dripping wet at the edge of the pool. Wouldn't hurt to do a little more digging, although he knew it would likely lead nowhere. "You know, Carlo," he began, "last night Kimberly was asking me where you were from and I realized that I didn't know, either."

Carlo smiled in reply. "Me? Oh, nowhere in particular. I've always moved around a lot."

"You have to be from somewhere," Max said with a friendly grin. If he could find out even that much about Carlo, it would be a place to start looking into his background. He still wasn't completely sure he wanted to put Kimberly in Carlo's hands in the bedroom later. If Max had *anything* else to go on, it would help in his decision, irrational as the decision seemed.

"Nope, always just moved around," Carlo replied, cheerful as ever. "Even when I was a kid."

"Where do your parents live?"

"No parents," Carlo answered simply.

From the corner of his eye, Max saw Kimberly sit up and adjust her lounge chair to the raised position. "No parents?" she said, leaning back.

Carlo shook his head. "Lost them both a couple of years ago."

Kimberly tilted her head. "Oh, I'm sorry. What happened to them?"

"They were old, both of them in a rest home," he said, and left it at that, as if dying parents were a very small thing.

"Still," Kimberly replied, "I know it's hard to lose a parent." At first Max thought she was trying to help him coax information from the guy, but what she'd just said finally hit him...

"You've lost your parents?" Carlo asked her across the pool.

She nodded. "My father died when I was very little. I don't remember him. But my mom died just a little over two years ago. She had cancer."

Max swung his head around to Kimberly, but she looked away. He hoped Carlo hadn't noticed his shocked expression, but he couldn't hide it. When he'd known Kimberly before, her mother had been alive and well. He'd only met the woman a few times, but she'd been a very nice lady and he knew Kimberly was close to her, being an only child.

"That was, um, two years ago in...?" Max asked uncertainly. He felt like an idiot to have to pose such a question in front of Carlo, but he felt like an even bigger idiot to be hearing the news like this, now, without being able to react.

"You remember, honey," she said, looking at him without really looking at him. "In February. Two years ago in February."

"Mmm, that's right." Max didn't know what else to say. Inside, his heart was bursting with sorrow for her and he wanted to show his concern, find out if she'd coped okay, do something to comfort her. But he couldn't, at least not right now.

He ran his hand back through his hair. Why hadn't she told him? Of course, when would she have? Well, maybe when she'd asked about his parents on the ride here two mornings ago, if he'd only been civil enough to ask about hers. He couldn't believe it. What a devastating loss for her.

"I'm sorry, Kimberly," Carlo said. Carlo, of all people, comforting her when it should be *him* comforting her. He stifled a groan of frustration.

Breaking the silence, she swung her feet to the patio and stood up. "Bathroom break," she announced. Max watched her slender form move away from him and into the house and he decided that he had to talk to her...now.

"I'm gonna grab some chips," he told Carlo, and he followed after her—his partner, his lover, his "wife." Oddly, it was starting to feel as if she was really all three of those things.

"Brandt!" he yelled after walking in the house and closing the French doors behind him.

"What?" she replied from the hallway.

"Wait up, I need to talk to you." He hurried through the kitchen and into the hall, where he found her lingering just outside the bathroom. He brought his face close to hers. "Why didn't you tell me?"

"Tell you what?"

"About your mother. I'm sorry, Kimberly. I know you were close to her."

She nodded, then glanced down, clearly not very comfortable with the topic. "Yeah, I was. And it was tough. But I got through it."

He nodded. His new, stronger Kimberly. Something about that strength made his stomach clench in a strange mixture of admiration and affection and also a little bit of fear. He just hoped the same sweet, gentle Kimberly he'd known before was still inside her, too.

He lifted a hand to her soft cheek, pinkened by the sun. "I just...wish you'd have told me. Wish I'd have known. I'd like to have been there for you or something."

Kimberly shook her head, looking incredulous at his sincerity, and he pulled his hand away. "When would I have told you? We haven't exactly been in touch. And you haven't exactly been much for small talk most of the time we've been here together."

She had him there. Knowledge of his heartless way of acting toward her made his stomach sink. He glanced down, feeling oddly ashamed. "I know. I'm sorry."

"Don't apologize, Tate. We're here on a job, not to socialize. But just don't expect to know every detail of my life." She looked him squarely in the eye. "I'm not the same girl you knew, Max."

"That's completely clear to me."

"Oh?"

"It's like you told me before. You're tougher."

Kimberly studied him. Was that a hint of appreciation in his eyes? Probably not. Still, she somehow got the impression that he approved of the person she'd become.

Now she only wondered what he'd think to know that some parts of her remained as soft as ever underneath it all. That, in fact, sometimes she wondered if all this toughness she wore now was truly genuine, really her, or if it was all a complete fabrication to cover up her weaknesses. He'd likely be disappointed, but that hardly mattered. He didn't really care for her anyway. Oh sure, maybe as a person—his concern right now over her mother's death demonstrated that—but it was a far cry from what she had going on in her heart for him and she knew it. So it was best not to start entertaining any thoughts to the contrary.

"Kimberly, I really am sorry about your mom." He lifted the same hand he'd used to touch her cheek and placed it on her shoulder, firm and comforting. She sort of wanted to collapse into his arms and quit being tough-girl Kimberly, but this was no time for that. Nor was this a man who really wanted that. *Be the employee he's paying you to be. Pull away from him.*

She shrugged free from his touch, hard as it was to make herself do it. "Thanks, Max." She felt uneasy, and she wanted to get away. "You know, I think I've had enough sun for today. I'm going to go shower and change."

He nodded. "I'll go hang out with Carlo some more, maybe grill some hamburgers for lunch." He glanced at a clock down the hall, so Kimberly followed suit. It was noon. "Two o'clock will be here before long."

Thank goodness, Kimberly thought. The sooner this was all over, the better.

"You're...sure you're ready to go through with the plan?" he asked her.

"Damn it, yes!" she snapped, stomping her bare foot on the hardwood floor. When would he ever start trusting her to do her job?

"All right, all right," he said, raising his hands in a calming gesture. "Don't get mad."

"I'm not. I just want you to quit questioning me on it, that's all."

"Okay, Brandt, whatever you want. No more questions."

"Good."

KIMBERLY STEPPED out of the shower, refreshed in body, but not in mind. She still hadn't managed to wash away the mounting pain of all she felt for Max but couldn't express.

Less than two hours, though, and this would all be through. Less than two hours and they'd have Carlo on film trying to steal her jewelry. She'd have proven herself to Max, once and for all. And then she could go home.

After that she could begin the business of trying to get over him again, which she knew from experience would be futile. She would always love Max, and she would always feel incomplete without him in her life.

She toweled off, then put on a summery, peach-flowered dress that buttoned up the front, hugged her shape and showed plenty of thigh and cleavage. She'd long since gotten bored with using her body to lure Carlo in—frankly, it hadn't taken much work—but most all the clothing she'd brought fell into that category. Besides, she had to wear something at least sort of sexy because she had to make sure Carlo wanted her this afternoon.

She blew her hair dry and pulled it back from her face into a pretty chignon, then applied a little makeup, noting that the warm colors of the dress and the bit of tan she'd picked up over the last two days combined to give her a tropical kind of look she found appealing. Maybe Max would, too. Not that it mattered, of course. His interest wouldn't go beyond her skin.

Well, back to work, she decided then. From outside the open balcony door, she could smell the hamburgers Max was grilling for lunch. She'd go down in a few minutes, but in the meantime, it might be a good idea to practice the combination and check out the jewelry again. After all, she'd gotten interrupted yesterday when she'd tried to do that and in less than two hours it was show time for real.

She padded across the carpet to the safe and spun the lock. Thirty, thirty-one, thirty-two.

Voila. It opened.

She reached inside and extracted the black velvet box. She'd seen it just hours ago, but it still had the ability to captivate her senses somehow, as if the jewelry inside was real, as if everything about this weekend was real.

But it's only pretend. Remember that, Kimberly. In less than two hours she would click her heels together and be returned to the Kansas that was her apartment, her real life, and all this would be nothing more than a dream. The only part that would count for anything would be that they would put Carlo Coletti—and hopefully his bosses, too—behind bars.

She lifted the box's lid and looked inside, the reflected colors of the shimmery fake jewels dancing in the sunlight that shone in from the balcony.

"Kimberly."

The voice came from behind her and caught her off guard.

Because it didn't belong to Max.

She turned as Carlo stepped into the room, wearing his swim trunks and a T-shirt, a lecherous grin beaming from his smarmy face. He fixed a hungry gaze on Kimberly, then closed the bedroom door.

8

ALL THE AIR drained from Kimberly's lungs. Her knees went weak, her throat dry.

She forced a smile and tried to make it shine through her eyes as well. "Carlo, what are you doing up here?" *What do you think you're doing coming into my bedroom without even knocking?* But she kept the question inside and held her smile firm.

"You promised to, uh, show me your jewelry today, remember? Looks like you were thinking about it, too." He glanced at the open velvet box in her hands.

"This isn't really the best time, Carlo," she pointed out gently. Where the hell was Max?

"Why's that, sweetheart?"

"Well, Max is right downstairs," she told him. "I thought we'd wait until later, that maybe I'd send him out to run some errands or something. Then you and I could have some...privacy." At this point she despised letting this sleazeball think she could want anything to do with him sexually, but under the circumstances, it was the only way she could think to handle the situation.

"Now, don't you worry about Max. It's just you and me here."

Carlo had made similar statements before, but for some reason, a bolt of panic rushed through her this time. He hadn't done anything to Max, had he? "Um, where *is* Max?" If he'd hurt Max, she would kill him! Brutally and without a shred of mercy.

"He's making lunch for us," Carlo said. "See?" He walked out onto the balcony, urging Kimberly to follow. Her heart flooded with relief to find Max, now in a pair of khaki shorts and a pullover shirt, standing at the grill flipping hamburgers.

"Well, don't you think he'll notice us missing?" she asked. "I mean, remember what happened the last time Max found you in here—he'll go ballistic."

"I told him I was going to use his office to make some phone calls," Carlo said, stepping back inside. Then he chuckled and took her hand. "So come on, baby, let's quit wasting time."

With one quick movement, he pulled Kimberly to him, making her drop the jewelry box. Fake diamonds scattered across the carpet. She braced her hands on his chest and took a step back, then swallowed hard. *What now?* she thought desperately. Break free of him and go running like a banshee from the room, screaming for Max? No, that would botch the whole assignment and it would prove to Max that she really *couldn't* handle her job. She had to find a way to bail herself out of this mess and keep the charade intact.

"Carlo, are you sure you wouldn't rather wait until later when we could...relax? Have more time? Go more...slowly?"

He pulled her back against him, tight. "Later sounds great, but nothing says we can't have a little warm-up right now."

Kimberly pushed against Carlo's chest again, but it was like being trapped in a vise.

"What's wrong? Don't play hard to get with me now. You've been hot for me since we laid eyes on each other."

Kimberly's stomach dropped. She hated the way he held her and she suddenly didn't feel nearly as much like a P.I. as she did a very vulnerable woman who'd gotten herself into a bad situation. Now she wasn't even sure that breaking away from him was an option—his grip on her was too strong.

"CARLO, how do you like your burgers? Well-done? Medium?"

No answer.

Max looked over his shoulder to where Carlo had been sunning by the pool just a moment ago. Damn it, he was gone.

And Kimberly was upstairs alone.

He dropped the metal spatula in his hand and ran across the patio and into the house, flinging the French doors wide. How had the little rat sneaked away so quietly? He raced through the family room and the foyer and took the stairs two at a time. Why hadn't he been paying closer attention, for God's sake?

He burst into the master suite out of breath, and just in time. He was ready to tear Carlo apart when he took in the scene before him. Carlo held Kimberly in what was clearly a forced embrace—her hands pressed flat against his chest as she leaned away from him as far as his grip would allow.

"Let go of her, Carlo!"

Kimberly gasped, then swung her gaze to where he stood in the doorway. "Max..." The utterance sounded unplanned and desperate, her eyes brimming with fear and something deeper. It was as if he could feel her reaching out to him, needing him.

He shifted his eyes to her for only the briefest of seconds before turning them back on Carlo, as enraged as a hungry tiger who'd just broken free of his cage. He clenched his fists so hard that his knuckles strained, his heart filling with such deep fury that he feared he might explode with it.

Crossing the room, Max grabbed Carlo by his shirt and spun him around, leaving Kimberly to flee to the nearest corner. She looked terrified of what lay ahead and maybe with good reason, too, he thought. Carlo hadn't actually done anything illegal yet, and if Max didn't find some way to rein in the anger taking hold of him, *he* might be the one going to prison.

"Max," Kimberly pleaded softly.

"Come on now, man," Carlo was saying, his hands held out before him. "Calm down."

But all Max could see was the fear and loathing in Kimberly's eyes when he'd walked in the room. He'd known he shouldn't let her go through with this and he'd been right. Now he finally understood why. She couldn't handle Carlo, and *he* couldn't handle watching her with Carlo. Both of them were too weak for the job, and even though their weaknesses lay in different areas, they had the same result.

Heedless of anything but his own wrath, Max pulled back his fist and landed it squarely on Carlo's left jaw. He wanted to kill the guy, wanted to make him suffer, not only for scaring Kimberly, but for each and every leer and touch he'd given her since the moment he'd walked in the door Friday night.

Regaining his balance after the blow, Carlo drew

back and threw an uppercut at Max, but he dodged it and caught Carlo's wrist in his grip. Max's other fist slammed into Carlo's face, knocking him backward into the wall.

Max didn't care about the case anymore—this wasn't worth it. It wasn't right that Kimberly, or any woman, should have to endure such mauling, even if it was for a good cause. Suddenly the cause wasn't good enough. *No* reason was good enough.

He closed in on Carlo, who stood cowering before him now, a surprised sort of panic invading his eyes. Clearly, he hadn't pegged Max as a guy who could fight, but since he chose not to carry a gun, Max considered a dexterity with his fists among his most essential skills.

The sight of Carlo looking so easily beaten did something to pacify him, though, and made him realize just how spineless a man he was dealing with. Carlo was more than anxious to prey on innocent women, but when it came to facing a man, someone of equal size and strength, he wasn't up to the challenge.

Their eyes met and held for a long, indecisive moment as Max waited to see the slimeball's next move. Max readied himself, just in case Carlo decided to come back at him. "What now, Carlo?" he asked, fists still clenched, eyes narrowed in threat. It was almost a dare.

Carlo's gaze darted past Max—to Kimberly, to the jewelry spread across the carpet, to the door—his eyes dancing with indecision.

It appeared that the door won out. "I guess now I leave," Carlo said, inching toward it. A certain smoothness had returned to his voice upon realizing Max wasn't going to beat him to a pulp.

Max moved slowly after him, almost sorry Carlo didn't want to have another go at him. "Which is harder to leave behind, Carlo?" he said, his voice still dripping with anger. "My wife or her jewelry?" He knew he came dangerously close to tipping their hand with that, but the words had tumbled out. Pride demanded he not let Carlo leave without letting him know they were onto him.

Carlo backed into the doorway. "Your wife," he replied snidely, clearly not realizing the question was rhetorical. He then turned a surprisingly smug gaze to Kimberly. "You don't know what you're missing, baby."

Max lunged for him, but if he'd intended to do Carlo real damage, he'd waited too long—the jerk had already slipped out the door and disappeared up the hall.

Instinct nearly made Max give chase, but several things kept him from it. Catching him would only mean pounding him into the ground—still a pleasing notion, but not particularly useful. As unimportant as the case had seemed a minute ago, it still mattered, and Max realized he'd just made a fatal error. Somehow in the tussle with Carlo, he'd managed to get their positions turned around so that he'd stood between Carlo and the jewelry. Carlo had just darted from the room without it, so besides having nothing on film, they didn't even have any stolen jewelry to report.

But the biggest reason he didn't go after Carlo in that moment was that it seemed much more important to make sure Kimberly was okay. Max turned toward her, finding her lips tightly pursed and her eyes filled with distress. He moved quickly to her side. "Are you all right?" He didn't wait for an answer before crushing her against him in a huge hug.

"Yeah," she murmured into his chest as she clung to him.

He released a long sigh at how good and safe it felt just to have her in his arms where no one could hurt her, where no one could touch her but him.

MAX AND KIMBERLY ran out the front door a minute later, just in time to see Carlo's Camaro flying up the wooded driveway that led from the house. They hopped into Max's Porsche and sped after him. Giving chase hadn't seemed important a moment ago, but as Max had stood there holding Kimberly, they'd both realized it would be their only chance to find out any more about Carlo.

After all, he had a boss somewhere who was expecting some jewelry. With any luck, that's where he would head right now. They'd blown the whole operation and this was their only chance to salvage it. "Hold on, babe. This is gonna be a wild ride," he said, swinging the car out onto the road.

Damn it! he thought, banging his hand on the steering wheel as he drove. He still couldn't believe this had happened, not any of it. How could he let Carlo slink away and get his hands on Kimberly like that? He also couldn't believe that after all the trouble they'd gone to, things hadn't come off as planned. The little creep had still managed to get away without doing anything illegal.

Max had thought the guy would lie back and let a

flirtatious, assertive woman do the work and make the plan, but he'd misjudged Carlo's ego. He was a better P.I. than that—he should have had a backup plan in place and kept a closer eye on the skunk. Damn all the distractions that kept making him mess up! Distractions caused over and over again by Kimberly.

The long chase led them across town and into the Garment District, an area rife with old warehouses and deserted buildings. Many of the structures harbored broken windows—some that had been boarded up, others that hadn't. The streets were pockmarked with holes and broken pavement. Now *this*, he thought, finally makes sense. The Garment District had Carlo's name written all over it.

He slowed his speed and hung back a bit as Carlo had suddenly slowed a little, too, since entering the rundown area. Apparently he had no idea he was being followed, the schmuck. It irritated Max to think that Carlo thought he and Kimberly were so helpless and stupid that they were back at the house crying over what had happened and not taking any action. And it made him more determined than ever to beat the guy at his own game.

"Look!" Kimberly said, pointing. Up ahead, Carlo had braked before one of the warehouses and turned into the driveway in front.

Max immediately pulled the Porsche to the side of the street, where they both watched in silence, although it was too far away to see much. Max reached under his seat to snatch a small pair of binoculars.

"What do you see?"

"He's punching something into a keypad, a code or password to get him inside," he guessed.

Then they both saw a large metal door rising, and Carlo drove through. The door promptly descended behind him.

"Damn," Max said, lowering the binoculars.

"Damn what?" Kimberly asked. "We know where he goes now. This is probably where the kingpins of the business operate."

Sure, that much was good news, but Max shook his head anyway. "We don't have anything on them. Still no hard, tangible proof. I've got to get something concrete, Kimberly. If we have any chance of nailing Carlo and whoever his bosses are, I've got to get inside that warehouse and take a look around, try to see what's going on."

Kimberly just gaped at him. "Are you crazy, Max? We have no idea what's behind those walls."

"Well, there's only one way to find out."

Max turned off the engine and opened his door, but Kimberly still continued to look at him as if he'd lost his mind. "This isn't safe, Max. I don't even know what you're planning, but I can tell you it's not safe."

"You wait here," he said, "and if I'm not back in half an hour, take the car and go get Frank." He pressed the keys into her hand.

But she was shaking her head at him, vehemently now. "You're not going in there, Max."

"Yes, I am."

She released a heavy sigh. "Well then, you're not going in there without me."

Max just looked at her. Kimberly. Sweet, brave Kimberly, whose ability to handle this situation he wasn't so sure he trusted, even now. And whose heart seemed so big, bigger than he'd ever realized before. He wanted to tell her there was no way in hell she was going inside that building with him, but they were partners on this case. She'd seen him through this far. If she really wanted to come, he didn't think he had any right to tell her she couldn't.

"Are you sure you want to do that?" he asked.

"Completely."

They got out of the car and walked up a cracked, neglected sidewalk toward the large building, hanging close to the warehouses they passed just in case Carlo or anyone else was on the lookout from inside. Nearly there, Max pointed out a single entrance at the corner of the structure near the freight door Carlo had gone through.

Next, Max pulled a small flip phone from the pocket of his khaki shorts. "I'm calling Frank," he said. "As a precaution."

A moment later, Frank's answering machine picked up, complete with soft blues music behind his friendly message delivered in a cool tone of voice. "Hi there. You've reached Frank Marsallis's personal line. Leave a message when the music ends."

"Frank, it's Max. It's Sunday afternoon, just after one o'clock. Kimberly and I have tailed our suspect to a warehouse on Lang Street in the Garment District, with a faded sign that says Dormer and Sons over the door. We're going in to take a look around. I'll call you when we're out, but if you don't hear from me... Well, just make sure you hear from me, okay?"

Flipping the phone shut, he shoved it in his pocket and began to have second thoughts about letting Kimberly go with him. A minute ago he'd been strictly in professional mode, thinking of Carlo and how to bring him and his people down, thinking of the job and the sometimes dangerous life of a P.I. in general. But this case, he had known from the start, *definitely* held danger. And the more time he spent with Kimberly, the less he was able to keep anything about it professional.

He turned to her as they walked. "Are you really absolutely sure you want to do this?" He tried to sound as casual as possible considering the weight of the question. "You might be of more use to me on the outside."

She looked deeply into his eyes before answering, and the warm, golden tone of hers struck him as both soft and incredibly bold at the same time. "I'm a better P.I. than you think, Max," she said very quietly.

The claim took him aback a little, made him feel sort of guilty. "Kimberly, despite the Carpenter case, I...think you're a fine P.I. Honest."

He'd started calling her Kimberly again, she realized, not Brandt. It was something she normally took little notice of one way or the other, but at the moment, it softened something inside her.

Still, she didn't think he sounded, or looked, truly convinced. And maybe it was silly at this point, but she still had the burning urge to show him, to prove to him, that she could work alongside him and do the same job he could and do it well. It was a matter of professional pride and it ran deep. In the beginning he'd been her mentor and then she'd let him down. What had happened back at the house just now with Carlo had made her feel as if she'd let him down again. She'd been unable to handle the situation, after all, and she'd been frighteningly close to crumbling. She had to make him see that she wouldn't let him down anymore.

"I intend to go, Tate."

He tilted his head and she waited for the argument she saw in his eyes, but he merely sighed. "All right, Brandt. All right."

A minute later, Max's hand rested on the doorknob and Kimberly stood behind him, ready to sneak in when the door opened. An eerie sense of danger bit into her spine. She'd told Max back in the car that this was crazy, yet here she was doing it herself, and it was too late to back out now.

"This would be easier in the dark," Max mused, "but we don't have that luxury. Stay low," he warned her. "When we get in, look for the nearest thing to hide behind and get there fast."

Max began easing the door open, peeking inside. Kimberly's heart beat a wild rhythm as pure fear gripped her, as she suddenly realized the full scope of what they were doing. What had seemed simply crazy a minute ago now seemed insane beyond description. Next, he took her hand and led her into the enormous warehouse where they could hear voices somewhere. He guided her silently across the floor until they were behind a forklift that held a pile of wooden crates.

Made it! Kimberly thought, but she didn't really know yet if that was true. Stealthily, she leaned around to peer past the crates and felt her first real sense of relief to see that no one had heard them, no one was running to see who had just come inside.

Then she looked at Max, who gave her a short, unexpected hug that quickened her pulse even as it somehow reassured her. She'd done plenty of unusual work since she'd joined the ranks as a P.I., but she'd never done anything like this before, and she'd also never done anything that made her feel as if she was in this deep.

Her only comfort was being in it with him. Despite her fears, she was glad she hadn't waited in the car—she wouldn't have been able to stand not knowing what was happening to him inside.

Max took her hand in his as they moved along the enormous outer wall of the building under the cover of crates and steel drums. She studied the place as they made their way. It didn't look like the office of some grand jewelry-theft ring. It looked like a normal warehouse, dim of light and stacked with slatted crates, the word Fragile stamped on their sides. Above her, aging rafters loomed, from which hung bare lightbulbs dangling at the end of old wires.

Yet Carlo had come in here. "Shipping," she suddenly whispered."

"What?" Max asked, just as soft.

"Carlo said he worked in shipping." She motioned to a stack of crates. "Maybe this is a legitimate business and he just works here."

Max looked skeptical. "I don't think so. He hightailed it here too fast. And besides, I just have a funny feeling—call it a P.I.'s sixth sense—that we're extremely close to some answers."

Over the last few years, Kimberly had developed that same sense herself, and despite her suggestion, she had to agree. In the distance, she still heard faint voices that reconjured her fears. She and Max were in real danger from more people than just Carlo.

"What now?" she whispered.

"Now we investigate a little."

It sounded impossibly dangerous. "How?"

Max pointed to a nearby crate on the floor. It looked neatly and recently packed, the top still open. "Let's see what these guys ship."

He silently reached inside and pulled out a heavy glass pitcher made of creamy white ceramic, the inside stuffed with wads of newspaper that would keep it from breaking in transit. Setting it aside, he dug through the straw in the crate, uncovering more of the same. But when he started to return the first pitcher, they both heard the slight jiggle in the bottom of it.

They looked at each other briefly before Max reached inside, gently pulling out the newspaper. When he uncrumpled it, Kimberly fought to hold in her gasp—a ruby-studded necklace lay nestled within the newsprint. "They must smuggle the stuff out in these things," Max whispered, "using the glassware as a front."

"What do we do with it?" she asked, her eyes still glued to the shimmering rubies.

Max hesitated, then stuffed both the newspaper and the necklace back inside the pitcher. "We leave it where we found it...for now. I'm not done investigating yet."

"But isn't this enough to take to the pol—"

He lifted two fingers to her lips, gently quieting her, and she quickly understood why.

"Beautiful stuff, isn't it?" The voice belonged to Carlo.

Kimberly froze, but soon realized that he wasn't talking to them—yet he stood just beyond the crates they now crouched behind, speaking with another man. She rose just enough to see several diamond necklaces dangling from the fingers of a paunchy, older guy next to Carlo.

"Sure is," the man agreed. "The boss is gonna love it."

Carlo laughed. "Now, you know the boss doesn't have an eye for this stuff. It's all just sparkly shiny money to him."

The fat man lowered his gravelly voice. "So, how'd *you* do this weekend?"

"Not so well," Carlo said with a sigh. "Guy caught me messing with his wife and I had to split. And you know the boss's golden rule—never let anybody see you take it. Couldn't swing that this time, so I came away empty-handed."

The other man shook his head. "The boss ain't gonna like that, Coletti. Your little habit of playin' around with rich wives cost you a heist."

Carlo gave an arrogant shrug. "It's the first time I've ever messed up. The boss shouldn't have any complaints about me."

"So," the man said, a toothy grin spreading across his face, "how *was* the woman?"

"Totally hot," Carlo bragged. "And totally crazy about me."

"How far did you get before you got caught?"

Carlo smiled. "All the way," he lied. "Even without any jewelry, it was worth the effort."

The two men snickered and, next to her, Kimberly felt Max go tense. She squeezed his hand to calm him. He returned the gesture and she didn't know if he'd gotten her silent message, but she liked the small, warm charge of energy it sent melting through her body even in the midst of danger.

After chatting a minute more, the two men went their separate ways, leaving the area quiet again. "What now?" Kimberly asked Max.

"We keep investigating."

"What else are we looking for? We already found some stolen jewelry."

But Max's reproachful glance said, *Be the P.I. you know you can be. Do what it takes to solve this case and bring these crooks down.*

"I'm ready," she said staunchly beside him.

"Ready for what?"

"Ready to investigate. Ready to do whatever it takes to send these guys to jail."

He blinked and looked at her, apparently having heard the return of the more capable Kimberly in her voice.

"Don't look so shocked, Tate," she said. "It doesn't become you." Then she studied the scene around them. "Now, I'm thinking that door over there looks like it might lead into an office of some kind. See the desk and file cabinet through the glass? I don't think anyone's in there. It might be a good place to locate some paperwork that could be used as evidence, or for keeping stolen property before it's packed up and smuggled out. What do you think?"

He grinned, clearly impressed. "I think you're right, Brandt."

Still holding hands, they cautiously made their way to the door Kimberly had indicated. After peeking around a barricade of steel drums, Max motioned her forward. She moved to the door and opened it, her heart beating frantically, then slipped inside. Max followed.

Together they began rifling through paperwork—Kimberly handling the cluttered beaten-up desk, Max digging in the file cabinet.

A moment later Max was by her side, silently pointing to a rumpled bill of lading clutched in his fist. She saw the skewed numbers instantly. Someone had paid Dormer and Sons over half a million dollars for a hundred vases!

"Not all the invoices are like this," Max whispered, his voice barely audible. "Some of their business must be legit. The rest they must run through their system, pushing it off as extremely expensive glassware."

Their eyes met in triumph, then Max folded the piece of paper and crammed it in his pocket, obviously ready to go to the police.

But it occurred to Kimberly to ask, "Crooks make out invoices for their stolen goods?"

Max shrugged. "I guess thieves need a way to track their profits just like anybody else, especially in an operation as big as this one appears to be. Now let's get out of here," he whispered.

They were making their way toward the office door when Max stumbled. The metal waste can he'd tripped over toppled with a metallic-sounding crash that echoed up from the concrete floor.

They both went as still as statues, their eyes going to the overturned can before raising to each other. They both knew the noise had been too loud and the timing couldn't have been worse. Kimberly could faintly detect voices coming from outside the office just beyond their view.

"Great stuff, Reggie," a deep-voiced man said. "Good work, as usual."

"Thanks, boss." It sounded like the paunchy man again.

"Boss, I just heard something." *This* voice, however, belonged to Carlo.

Max and Kimberly exchanged glances full of dread, but before they could even move, the office door burst open.

9

CARLO STOOD before them with the big man, Reggie, as well as an older guy whom Max took to be the boss. His craggy face gave an impression of age combined with experience. He was clearly a gangster, through and through.

"Who the hell are these people?" he asked.

"These are the two I just spent the weekend with." Carlo looked Max squarely in the eye and shook his head, his voice deadly serious. "Maxxy boy, you made yourself a big mistake by coming here. And bringing Kimberly?" He continued to shake his head. "Bad move, Max."

Max didn't reply, but Carlo's words echoed in his heart. Bringing Kimberly here had indeed been a very bad move. Damn it. Why did he have to trip over that waste can? He sighed, tired and worried—it didn't matter now. What mattered was that they'd been caught.

"I don't know why you followed me, Max, if you were trying to play the big hero for your wife or what, but I can promise you this. You just got yourself in deeper trouble than you ever even imagined could exist."

"You know what to do, boys," the boss said then,

and as Carlo and Reggie started toward them, Max realized that he was far from giving in.

"Run, Kimberly!" he said.

The next thing Max knew, Kimberly had picked up an old black telephone from the desk and flung it at Carlo, dinging him in the head and knocking him back a few steps.

Then he found himself wrestling with Reggie, who—stronger than he looked—succeeded in shoving Max backward onto the desk. Fortunately, the position gave Max leverage and he managed to get to his feet even as he threw a right to Reggie's stomach, then a left to his eye.

He saw his cell phone skitter across the floor amid the fight, and then heard Kimberly's voice. "Back here, Tate!"

A quick look over his shoulder revealed that she'd found another door at the rear of the office. He could only assume if she was calling him toward it that it was more than a closet. Reggie was recovering his balance now and Max just eluded his grasp, circling the desk and running through the door, which led back out into the warehouse through a pathway lined with steel drums.

"Run, Kimberly! I'll catch up!" he yelled.

It took a few precious seconds and all the strength Max possessed, but he managed to haul down one of the huge drums to send it rolling toward his pursuers. After a few more steps, he brought a crate crashing down, shattering a mountain of dishes in the path.

Max's heart beat a mile a minute by the time he found Kimberly huddled behind yet another row of crates. "Don't make a sound," he warned her in a near-silent whisper.

Every nerve in Kimberly's body was tensed and ready for action. Daring to peek around the wall of boxes that currently protected them, she saw Carlo and the old boss man across the way. Carlo carried a gun.

"Find them!" the boss exploded. "Now!"

They hadn't been seen yet, but this was definitely not a good enough hiding place. Obviously thinking the same thing, Max spoke to her in a barely discernible whisper. "As soon as the three of them get a little farther away, we make a run for it. Follow me."

She nodded.

"Let's go," he said a moment later, and they scurried quietly from their hiding place, ducking between another row of boxes and crates, passing behind a forklift, hand in hand.

Suddenly, an order blared over a loudspeaker. "Attention. We have two trespassers on the premises. Find them immediately!"

The voice clearly belonged to the boss and the announcement meant there were more than just the three men in the building with them. Maybe a *lot* more.

Max yanked Kimberly down behind the row of crates toward the other side of the warehouse until they reached the end of the aisle. When Max cursed softly, she glanced up to see that more seedy-looking men had just appeared. A group of four stood conferring in a circle.

Before Max and Kimberly could backtrack, they were spotted. "Hey, you there!"

Kimberly followed Max as he pulled her frantically across the floor. She had no idea where they were headed, and no other choice than to simply trust Max's instincts.

"Hold it!"

"Come back here!"

The voices behind her were close, too close, as she tried to keep up with Max.

"You can't get away, Max!" Carlo yelled.

Without warning, Max flung Kimberly aside and turned to face Carlo and his henchmen head-on. "You want to make a bet!" He leaped behind a mountain of crates and gave a mighty heave, sending them all toppling before the encroaching men, blocking their path with a loud crash of splintering wood and breaking glass.

He placed his hand back in Kimberly's and they started running, running, until they came to a large steel door. Max ripped it open and Kimberly turned instantly heartsick to see that it wasn't an exit, but a large closet.

"In here," Max said anyway.

She rushed in and Max followed, shutting the big door behind them, then pulling her behind a stack of boxes.

They both stayed quiet and stood close as their breathing began to slow.

Kimberly couldn't help leaning into him, and he rested his back against the cinder-block wall, hugging her, warm and tight and long.

Outside, footsteps finally faded and gradually she began to feel that they were safe, at least for right now.

Then Max's strong hands began to move, slow and comforting, easing over her shoulders and back. It was good and soothing simply to be in his embrace, simply to let him console her that way.

A long, silent moment later, when he began to pull her closer, his caresses growing slightly deeper, Kimberly realized they were on the verge of edging into a desperate, slow-burning passion that could only escalate. As his touch skimmed over her hips and then higher, she came to her senses. "Max."

"What?" he whispered, one hand at the side of her breast.

"What are you doing?"

"Touching you." His voice was raspy and sexy, which made protesting considerably harder, yet...

"Max, are you crazy? Think about where we are. We've got to figure out what to do."

Slowly, he lowered his hand. "You're right," he whispered. "I'm sorry, babe. I was a little...out of my mind." He ran his fingers through his dark hair.

"It's okay," she said, hands at his chest. "But we've gotta keep our heads here."

He nodded, and they went silent, his grip tightening on her waist, when muffled voices could suddenly be heard again nearby.

"Where the hell could they be? They didn't just disappear into thin air."

"All the entrances are being guarded, so they couldn't have gotten out."

Kimberly and Max tensed, their gazes meeting, as yet another voice joined the fray. "Any luck?"

"Nope, but the boss said to scour every nook and cranny until we find 'em. They gotta be here somewhere."

Max didn't like how close those voices sounded, almost as if they were in the same room. Dropping to his knees, he pulled Kimberly gently down beside him to better hide them behind the tall row of boxes.

Then he heard the door open.

And the vague, soft sounds of someone stepping inside, looking around.

He squeezed Kimberly's hand. He didn't like how afraid he was. Not afraid for himself. Afraid for her.

His heartbeat thundered in his chest. He waited for the door to shut again, for the relief to flood him, for them to be safe once more. Seconds seemed like hours.

But then he felt it. The unmistakable sensation of being seen. The silence did nothing to relieve the sensation, to make him think he was imagining it. Instead, it only intensified everything.

Dread filled him as he shifted his gaze to the left and up over the wall of boxes. Carlo's eyes peered back. He wore a leering grin. "Hi there, Max."

Max's chest tightened as he tensed for a fight, but then he remembered. Carlo had something he didn't—a gun—and Carlo chose just that moment to hold it up for Max to see.

Max got to his feet and Kimberly clambered up to stand slightly behind him, as Carlo and another guy stepped around the boxes so that no barrier stood between them.

"All right," Max said. "You win. Just let us go and we won't tell anybody about this place."

Carlo chuckled. "You think it's that easy?"

No, of course he didn't, but it had seemed like something he at least had to try.

"The boss had to leave, but this looks like a safe enough spot for you until he gets back tomorrow morning," Carlo said, looking around the closet. "No way out but the way in. And we'll be sure you don't get out *that* way, so don't even try."

"What's gonna happen when the boss gets back?" Max asked.

Carlo lifted the gun again, this time leveling it at Max. "Bang, bang," he said with a hideous smile.

Max felt all the blood drain from his face, but kept his voice steady when he asked, "What about Kimberly?"

Carlo's gaze shifted admiringly to her and he gave his head a regretful shake. "If it was up to me, I'd find some other way to deal with her. But it isn't. The boss isn't one for taking chances."

Carlo and his buddy went out and closed the door, locking them inside. Max instinctively pulled Kimberly tight against him. Neither of them said a word. This was a high-stakes operation and they knew Carlo wasn't exaggerating. Kimberly slid her arms around his neck and they embraced.

"What now, Max?" she whispered, feather-soft in his ear.

He considered their options as he continued to hold her—there weren't many. "I'm not sure," he admitted, releasing a long sigh and lifting a consoling hand to her cheek. "But it looks like we may as well get comfortable."

HOURS PASSED and hunger mounted. Max decided that if they made it through this, he was going to take Kimberly out for a lavish dinner someplace expensive. But for now, he tried not to mention food—God knew he was thinking about it, but if she wasn't, no need to make her start.

Each time he thought about making a run for it, he remembered Carlo's gun and the talk of guarded entrances and it made him stay put. He didn't like just waiting around, especially after a threat like the one Carlo had issued, yet who knew how many men were out there waiting for them to make the mistake of showing themselves?

And just where was Frank? Enough time had passed that his old mentor should have come looking for them by now, hopefully with the police in tow. But then, who knew how often Frank picked up his messages? Anything could have happened—his machine could have malfunctioned, or he might simply have missed the blinking light when he'd come in.

Now he and Kimberly sat side by side, their backs against the closet wall, both lost in private thoughts. Everything around them was quiet and had been for some time.

"I'm sorry, Kimberly," he suddenly felt compelled to say.

Even through the dim lighting in the closet, he saw her turn to look at him. "Sorry? For what?"

"Sorry you're in this mess with me. Sorry I didn't make you stay outside. Sorry I kicked over that trash can."

"Let's get something straight here, Max. I'm in this mess with you because it's my job to be. I know you don't have much faith in me professionally, but there's nothing you could have done to make me wait for you outside."

I'm glad it's you I'm here with, he wanted to say. *Good*

P.I., bad P.I., none of that matters now. Instead, he only sighed, and reached out to take her hand. "Kimberly?"

"Yes?"

"Tell me about...the Carpenter case."

Kimberly nearly went numb. He'd said it slowly, as though it would be as hard for him to hear as it would be for Kimberly to tell. But he was giving her the chance now, the chance to finally explain what had happened on that ill-fated day. She took a deep breath and tried to think of where to begin.

"Well, I found out my mother was dying on the day I blew the case," she started. From the corner of her eye, she saw him turn to look at her, but she kept talking. "She called me around noon to tell me she'd been diagnosed with cancer. I wasn't supposed to meet with Margaret Carpenter until later that afternoon, and I was just taking it easy in my apartment, letting Margaret think I was at work. So I got off the phone and rushed out the door to go be with Mom, but my cat got out into the hallway."

"Misha?" he said, stunning Kimberly once more by recalling the name of her cat.

She nodded. "I'd already locked the door, and I was frazzled and not thinking straight—in too much of a hurry to stop and put her back inside. I saw my neighbor, Mrs. Baines, coming in, and she said she'd catch Misha and take her to her place. I figured I'd get her when I came home before going to meet Margaret. Nothing really mattered besides seeing my mom right then, you know?"

"Of course." He spoke quietly and squeezed her hand.

"When I got to her house, we both cried and it

was…emotional. I wished I could've stayed longer and even thought about calling Margaret to reschedule, but Mom insisted I go on and do my job. So I headed home to change and when I got there—" she swallowed hard and forced the rest out "—I found out Misha had run away."

"Oh, Kimberly," he murmured.

It struck her funny that the memory of her cat disappearing came closer to causing tears now than the part about her mother, but, like then, it was the culmination of the events happening all at once that had the ability to make her feel so weak and helpless.

She took a deep breath and forged ahead. "Apparently, Mrs. Baines had trouble catching her—Misha was always afraid of strangers—and when one of the other tenants left the building, Misha ran out. Mrs. Baines tried to follow her, but Misha crossed the street and disappeared into the woods. I went into the woods myself and looked for her, called for her, but she was just…gone. After a while, I had to give up, and pull myself together enough to go meet Margaret."

Now Max was running his thumb lightly back and forth over the top of her hand. "You should have canceled with her, babe," he said sweetly.

"I know that now. Believe me, I know it. But at the time, I was on autopilot. Still reeling from the news about my mom and just pushing my way through the day, trying to get to the end of it, I guess." Kimberly paused and took another deep breath, remembering the overload of emotions.

"So I went to Margaret's, ready to work. But Margaret…well, despite what you may think, Max, she was a very kind woman. She saw immediately that I wasn't myself and asked what was wrong. A part of me knew I shouldn't tell her, but I truly liked her and at the time I really needed a shoulder to cry on, so I told her about my mother, and about what had happened to Misha, too." She gave her head a quick shake. "Of course, I had to make up a stupid story about Misha being my friend's cat and not mine, or Misha would have been there with me at the bungalow. Having to lie in the middle of all that didn't help.

"Anyway," she went on, not daring to lift her gaze to Max, "Margaret listened to me, and when I looked into her eyes, I knew she really cared. She even held me while I cried."

Max sighed, his eyes lowered.

"Then her son came in."

"Our client," Max said.

She nodded, hardly caring about that fact. "I could tell immediately that Margaret was afraid of him. Like I'd told you before, Bruce was gruff when he spoke to her. He didn't even knock on the door of her little house—just barged right in. And he ignored *me* completely. I was already so upset that seeing how he treated her made me angry." In fact, even just recalling it made anger well in Kimberly all over again.

"Margaret was clearly living on a shoestring, something I started thinking about while her son was there, and it helped me get back in a working frame of mind. After he left, I finally got down to business. I talked about the money she wanted to invest and asked her where she'd gotten it. She told me that she'd saved a little here, scrimped a little there. I said, 'Your son doesn't help you out with the bills?' She said, 'No, I just have what I get from Henry's social security.'

"And then...then I noticed these bruises on her arm, mainly because they were like fingerprints, like someone had grabbed her too hard. I asked her about them and she blushed and looked away, started fiddling with the doily on the table next to her. When I pressed her for an answer she told me that her son had done it. She told me they'd argued and he'd pushed her. She tried to play it off like it was no big deal, but I couldn't see it that way."

Pausing then, Kimberly clenched her fists, readying herself for the next part, the hardest part.

"That's when I cracked, Max. I quit caring about the case and started caring more about Margaret. I told her the truth about why I was there, why I had gotten to know her. I know it was wrong. I know it was stupid. And I regret it more than anything I've ever done. It was the biggest mistake of my life. It cost me my job. Worse, it cost you yours and you had nothing to do with it."

She turned to face him then, surprised and comforted that he still held her hand. Their faces were close. "I'm so very sorry, Max. I was so wrong to let my emotions get in the way of what I was there to do."

Finished, Kimberly waited for him to turn cold, or at least cool. That's how it had been on the day they'd gotten fired. It's how Max had reacted a few days ago when she'd tried to explain. Now she finally *had* explained, and it suddenly hit her—her excuse wasn't very good. Her emotions had gotten in the way? How utterly lame. How completely unprofessional.

"I understand," Max said softly, slowly, as if amazed by his own words.

But he couldn't have been any more amazed than Kimberly was. "You do?"

He gave a short nod. "Maybe I couldn't have understood it before, even if I'd let you explain it all to me. I can understand *now*, though, because I'm guilty of the same thing, guilty of bringing my emotions into *this* case." He lowered his voice. "Emotions for you."

Kimberly's stomach clenched. Was he talking about lust again? Or was there something else, something more?

"I owe you an apology, Kimberly," he went on. "For the times when I got angry with you this weekend. I put you in a tough position making you sexual bait for Carlo. Turns out everything you did to reel him in worked on me instead. I haven't been very professional over the last couple of days, and I was wrong to take out my frustrations on you. But I just wanted you so badly and it was so hard to watch him touching you, and you giggling with him and encouraging him."

She swallowed. She still wasn't really sure how he felt inside, if it was all merely sex or if there was anything else behind his desires. "It was my job, Max," she reminded him.

"I know," he told her, "and that's why I'm apologizing. You were doing your job and I started acting as if you were doing something wrong." He paused and turned toward her, their eyes meeting in the semidarkness. "Maybe the truth is that I expected you to do a worse job at being a seductress. I thought it would bother you more...maybe I *wanted* it to bother you more."

"It bothered me plenty, but I've gotten better at my job over the past three years."

"I've noticed." To her surprise, he gave her a small grin. "As we've discussed before, you're considerably sassier than I recall."

She shrugged. "I found out I had to be a little tougher if I wanted to survive in this business."

"It works for you," he said. "But..."

"But what?"

"But I like the *other* you, too, Kimberly. The *softer* you."

Something in Kimberly's stomach rippled. *He liked the softer her*, the her that she thought of as the *real* her. She wanted to succumb to his gentle words, to simply melt inside, but she thought that perhaps, at the moment, it would be smarter to concentrate on business lest she crumble completely. "I guess this has all proven, though, that tough or not, I'm not a very good P.I."

She felt his incredulous look. "Why would you say that?"

"Because in the end, when it mattered the most, I panicked and caved in—I messed up. I was afraid of him and I let him see that." She was remembering the moment she'd called Max's name when he'd burst into the room and saved her from Carlo, how it had tumbled from her lips unbidden, how desperate and afraid and needful she'd felt all at once. No matter how perfect the sight of him had been, it was an unprofessional move.

Yet Max was reaching up and smoothing her hair with gentle fingers, saying words she'd never thought she'd hear him say. "Some things are more important than a case, Kimberly. And I hate that I let you do that, that I let you be in that position with him."

"It's not an uncommon thing for a female P.I. to have to do, Max. You know that."

He sighed. "Of course I know that, but it's different—and a lot easier—when it's someone you don't know very well, someone you don't care for."

Kimberly's body suddenly felt as if it belonged to someone else, as if, piece by piece, it was shattering in a frightening bliss that it was far too soon to feel. *Stop it,* she commanded herself. *You're misunderstanding him. You must be.* Tears threatened to leak out, but she held them back. "You...care for me, Max?"

He released a huge sigh and then his arms were coming around her, drawing her close, holding her against him like something cherished. "Kimberly," he whispered, "do you really have to ask?"

She pulled back just enough to meet his eyes. "Well, yes, I do have to ask. I mean, after we slept together, Max, you...well, you acted..."

Max was silent as he leaned toward her until his forehead rested on her shoulder. "I know," he said. "I'm sorry for how I acted. I didn't want to admit to myself how I felt, how I cared. But I *did,* Kimberly. So much that it caught me off guard, scared me."

She swallowed at the impact of his words. That sounded serious. So serious that she couldn't delve any deeper right now, couldn't risk finding out it wasn't really true, that it meant something less than what she was hearing. So she kept it simple and asked him the question that had haunted her for days. "Max?"

"Hmm?" His head still rested on her shoulder.

"Who is Julie? A...lover?"

He lifted his head and smiled at her with a short, low laugh. "Julie lives next door to me. I pay her to clean my condo and do my laundry. She's sort of like a second mother to me."

"But you came out in a towel, thinking I was her."

Again, he laughed quietly. "She's seventy years old, Kimberly, and believe it not, she's seen me in a towel, even less—she nursed me through a killer stomach infection with a fever of 103 degrees last winter. She was supposed to drop my laundry off that night you came by." He gave his head a sly tilt, accompanied by a wicked little grin. "Were you jealous?"

She smiled at him as she lied. "No."

She knew he could see right through her, but that was okay, because they were sharing a moment, something quiet and without need of words. She still didn't know how he really felt for her, after all, he'd said wonderful things, but he'd not exactly confessed to loving her. Yet, even so, it just felt good to know there was *something* mutual between them, that it was not all one-sided, and most of all, it was incredible to know he understood now about the Carpenter case, and that he might even begin to forgive her.

Just in time, too, she thought, her mood suddenly going grave. For at any other place or any other time, this conversation would have been a dream come true, but recalling the reality of their situation hung a dark cloud over Kimberly's joy. Sadly, her confession to Max and his sweet, even if unexpected, understanding, may have taken place at the last possible moment it could.

Max tilted his head, studying her expression, which had just turned troubled, yet he didn't have to ask why. For a few moments there, it had been as if they'd forgotten, but the fact was, they might very well die tomorrow, something that he was just now fully comprehending. This wasn't a comic book, not pretend...this was real. He could only guess that it was hitting Kimberly just as hard.

He lifted one hand to her cheek. "I'm so sorry, Kimberly," he said. It still helped nothing, of course, but at least it came from the heart.

Yet she peered into his eyes and shook her head. "No, Max, truly, don't be sorry. Because it's not your fault. And because I'm not giving up yet. I refuse to believe this is over."

Even amid their suddenly remembered dread, he managed a small smile for her. "This is that tough, sassy side of you I like."

Max saw heat in Kimberly's gaze, a heat he recognized, a heat now tempered with a primitive sort of fear.

His heartbeat increased as he let himself be absorbed into those pretty eyes of hers. In the shadowy light of the closet, they were so dark as to be almost colorless. Yet they still shone hot upon him, and he could see in her all he ever had, all the beauty, all the grace, all the sweetness, all the raw sexuality, now magnified with the need that accompanied it.

Max couldn't wait another second. He crushed a hard kiss onto her silken lips, and she returned it, wild and needful, her arms twining around his neck as she leaned fully into him, her warmth intoxicating.

They were kissing desperately and she climbed into his lap, straddling him until his hardness pressed up into that most tender part of her. "I need you, babe," he murmured.

A small, reckless moan left her, but he stifled it with

another kiss, his tongue pressing hungrily past her lips. Their kisses turned less frantic then, calming into something deep and enveloping, slower, but still just as wrenching.

"I need you, too, Max." Her words were the merest whisper, like a verbal caress. "I need you so much."

They touched tongues delicately and Max slid one hand to her breast. Finding her nipple through her dress and bra, he gently squeezed it between thumb and forefinger. Another tiny moan came, but he cut this one off with his mouth, afraid someone might hear them.

He still teased the taut peak with rhythmic strokes of his thumb, and they were both panting now, quiet and harsh. Max feared he would soon burst with the intensity of how he wanted her. How his body *needed* her. But it wasn't just his body. No, this was way more than physical.

"Remember before," he said, short of breath, "when we stopped? Because of where we were?"

She nodded, their gazes seductively close, her eyes wide with want.

"Well, where we are doesn't matter anymore, Kimberly," he told her. "Or maybe it's just the opposite and it matters more than anything. Either way, nothing could stop me from having you now."

10

MAX HAD NEVER WANTED anyone or anything in his life as badly as he wanted to make love to Kimberly, right now. The feel of her, the scent of her, was enough to bury him.

She answered his words with a feverish kiss, but he wanted more than that from her. "Tell me," he growled in her ear.

"Tell you what?" she uttered.

"Tell me you want me inside you."

She released an erotic sigh and her voice came weak and breathy. "Yes, I want you inside me. I want you deep, deep inside me."

Then she looked hard into his eyes, voracious with desire, but also commanding, saying, *Don't play any more games, don't ask me to say anything else. Just do it.* Her silent demands excited him more than anything he could ever remember.

He moved his hands to her hips and pulled her down to meet him, drinking in the hungry sexiness of it when she began to grind against him in a hard, sensual rhythm. He worked at the buttons on her dress as she moved, then pushed the flowered fabric aside. Opening the lacy bra, he reached in to caress her full, round breasts. When she began to release a low moan, he kissed her and a passionate moment later felt her biting his lip.

And then *he* wanted to moan and it killed him to hold it in. So he clenched his teeth and closed his eyes and leaned his forehead against hers, all while she gyrated against him in hot little circles.

"I need you in me."

The words sounded as gentle as a leaf wafting from a tree, but the power in them was enough to paralyze him. He needed to be in her, too...as soon as possible. Grazing his hands over her thighs and up under her dress, he found more lace beneath his fingertips. Smoothly, he slid his fingers inside the fabric, taking hold of it. Then he gave one brisk yank, ripping the lace free. Her gasp filled him with a perverse sort of pleasure before he whispered, "Unzip me."

Her ragged breath alone was enough to drive him wild as she lifted off him and undid his shorts. "Hurry," he urged, his own voice sounding so throaty he barely recognized it. She reached inside and took hold of him, and he let out a rough gasp of his own.

He waited, impatient as a teenager, but she went still and looked him in the eye. He reached up to brush a strand of hair from her face. When she finally spoke, her voice came out broken. "Max, there's nowhere...no one else I'd rather..."

He couldn't stand to watch her struggle with the words, so he stopped her with a truth of his own. "I know, love. Me, too."

And then she was lowering herself onto him, taking him deep inside her. She released another of those long, low moans, and Max reached up to cover her mouth with his hand, quieting her.

His fingers were in her mouth then and she was sucking them, and she was moving on him again, now with him in her. Max began to lose track of space, time, reality. All he knew was that Kimberly had taken control and was making love to him. Sweet, slow, desperate love. Using her whole body, her whole self, her undulations filled with a smoldering hunger he'd never seen in her before. He basked in it, letting it happen, watching her love him, pushing up into her, wanting her to feel it deep in her core.

Biting her lip, she arched toward him, her lovely coral-tipped breasts near his face. He took one pebbled nipple in his mouth as she continued in those slow, sexy circles...and then he felt her coming—her body convulsing over him, around him, her sweet tiny sounds too faint to need to cover, too beautiful to want to. She collapsed against him and he wrapped his arms around her, thinking, *You're so beautiful,* when he came, too, in shocking waves of heat that made him shudder against her limp body. "Oh God, babe," he whispered, breathless.

"I love you, Max," she said.

He tightened his hold on her, not ready to hear those words, yet at the same time, he let his heart fill with them.

He didn't say it back. He felt stunned and speechless.

Max just prayed that she understood, prayed that she knew how much he felt in this moment, prayed that it would be enough to get her—to get them *both*—through the night.

And at the same time, he prayed desperately that there would be a tomorrow.

AT SOME POINT, they both slept. He awakened her with kisses—kisses to her shoulder, to the curve of her breast. She climbed onto him again in the small confines of the space, and she stayed faultlessly quiet, but he thought he could almost feel the exquisite torture of her silence as she moved against him.

Hours later, he awoke blissfully satisfied. Before even opening his eyes, he found himself ruminating about the other morning after they'd made love. In his mind he saw her dreamy eyes and romantic expression next to him in bed. He hadn't been ready for it then, but he was ready for it now. After what they'd been through together in the last twenty-four hours, he felt closer to her than he ever had. And on top of it all, he'd forgiven her for the Carpenter case.

He didn't know how or when exactly, but somehow through the course of the day yesterday, he'd let go of his hurtful grudge. He wished he'd told her now, before they'd made love. Even if he hadn't been able to say "I love you," "I forgive you" might have been almost as good under the strange circumstances of their relationship. He knew he needed to get better at saying how he felt, but he decided he'd work on that as soon as they got out of this. Right now he had other things to concentrate on.

Like figuring out what they were going to do.

And before that, waking Kimberly and drinking in that dreamy look in her morningtime eyes. But it wasn't quite morning yet—his digital watch read 4:30 a.m. Still, he didn't want them sleeping any later—if they were to formulate any kind of a plan, they'd better start working on it now. He nudged her softly and waited as she slowly lifted her head from his shoulder and eased her eyes open. Then she turned to him and met his gaze.

"Jeez, Tate, did you have to rip off my panties?"

Max flinched, stunned. Okay, that wasn't exactly dreamy or romantic. Maybe he didn't know Kimberly as well as he thought he did—she was becoming less predictable by the day. "Well, you didn't seem to mind it at the time," he pointed out.

"I was feeling…a bit desperate."

"Has your situation changed in some way I don't know about?"

Kimberly's situation hadn't changed, but her attitude definitely had. After last night with Max, it would have been easy for her to wake up feeling all lovey-dovey toward him, but she knew a lot about herself and one thing she knew for sure was that lovey-doveyness would make her weak and spineless and girlish. If they were to stay alive, she needed her professional wits about her today. So she'd decided to put on her game face bright and early without giving her spongier side time to start absorbing everything she felt when she looked in his eyes. Max had said yesterday that he liked her tough side. Well, today that's what he would get. It was imperative if they were to have any hope of getting out of this mess with their lives.

"We need a plan, Tate."

"I'm fresh out at the moment, Brandt."

"Well, I'm not. Listen up." Her change in attitude had imbued her with a strength she hadn't thought she'd be able to muster under the current circumstances. She surprised even herself with how bold she felt at the moment.

"I'm listening," he said.

"There's a heat duct overhead." She pointed at it.

"True enough."

"And so I'm thinking...what if we could somehow crawl through it and get out? They do it in the movies all the time."

"I don't know, Brandt—this isn't a movie. And that thing looks like it was manufactured in the Dark Ages. I think Hollywood uses sturdier heat ducts."

"Maybe so, but do you have any better ideas? Besides, it's the middle of the night. Carlo and his goons might have let down their guard, expecting us to be asleep. If we're gonna do something, it seems like now's the time."

Max tilted his head as he stared at her in the pale light. "That's your plan?"

"My point is, Tate, we can stay here and wait for Carlo's boss to shoot us, or we can take a chance in the heat duct. I say we go now and be done with it, one way or the other."

Max didn't like it, he was generally a planner. After all, a little spontaneity on his part is what had landed them in this predicament. Still, she made sense. There was nothing to be gained by waiting and the cover of darkness sure couldn't hurt. The rusty heat duct looked as if it was ready to disintegrate on top of them, but it seemed to be their only hope.

"All right, Brandt. You've convinced me."

"One more thing," she said. "Another part of my plan."

"Let's hear it."

"If we end up out of the heat duct and on the floor, and we bump into just one guy, split up."

"Where the hell is the logic in that?"

"One person can't shoot both of us at the same time."

Max *really* didn't like this. If they were going to get shot at, he had every intention of making sure he was the one who took the bullet.

"And," she added, "the guy will probably be keeping his gun stuffed in his pants behind his back, right? If one of us could possibly get behind him—"

Okay, he was crazy about the woman, but... "Brandt, that's too far-fetched. Like I said before, this isn't a movie."

"It's not far-fetched at all," she corrected him. "I saw Carlo pull his gun from there when we were out in the warehouse."

Max sighed, almost as if conceding. "Okay, so you've impressed me with your observational skills. Still, if we get caught, we stick together. No arguments."

She scowled at him, but he didn't care.

"Got it?"

Hesitantly, Kimberly nodded, but she let him see the irritation in her eyes.

He took a deep breath. "Ready to do this?"

She nodded again. "Although frankly, Tate, I'd feel better if I had underwear on."

This time *he* scowled. They exchanged looks of annoyance then, just like old times, Kimberly thought strangely.

They rose and Max carefully climbed up on a tower of boxes toward a metal slat in the duct that was partially disconnected from the rest, the screws missing.

After a few minutes of working at it, it finally came off completely, opening a hole to the duct.

"I'll go first," Max announced, and Kimberly knew he was thinking about protecting her. If the vent was going to come crashing down beneath the added weight, he wanted to be the one to fall, not her.

While her P.I.'s sensibilities were slightly offended, her feminine ones were not, so she simply said, "Okay," and watched as he pulled himself up into the duct with the agility of a cat. He disappeared inside and the duct didn't move or even sag, and she hoped that meant it was stronger than it looked.

Next, Kimberly followed Max's path up the boxes and into the duct. It wasn't easy in a dress, but soon she was in the pitch-black tunnel on her hands and knees.

She reached out a hand to make sure Max was still there...and found his butt.

"Jeez, Brandt. Not now."

"Quit dreaming," she snipped. "It was an accident."

"Are you in? Are we ready to crawl?"

"More than ready. Let's get going."

The going was slow and uncomfortable. Breathing was difficult. Although she could see nothing, she could smell, taste and feel the heavy dust particles all around her. Moving through the unrelenting blackness was nearly unbearable, but Kimberly tried not to feel claustrophobic and not to think about the possibility that bugs or vermin could be sharing the space with them.

"You all right?" Max asked after a little while.

"Yes," she lied, when she was really thinking, *Get me out of here!* Remembering that this was a life-or-death situation helped her focus on staying calm.

"Damn," Max whispered in front of her a few minutes later.

She didn't have to ask why. She'd already caught sight of the rectangle of dim light ahead.

"The duct is ending," he told her anyway. When he approached the end a moment later and peered down, he announced, "We're right in the middle of the damn warehouse."

Kimberly simply took a deep breath. "At least we're out of the closet," she reminded him.

"Good point," he answered over his shoulder. "We're gonna have to get down to the floor somehow, Brandt. And then we're gonna have to find our way out, quick and quiet. Ready?"

"After all this, I guess I'm ready for anything."

Kimberly watched as Max squeezed his legs around and out of the duct. Carefully he dropped himself down to the floor. He made the ten-foot jump gracefully and landed with barely a noise.

"Max," she whispered down to him. "I can't do that like you just did. I'll break my legs."

Below her, he was shaking his head and looking annoyed. "This is no time to go soft on me, Brandt. Just do it. Don't think about it. I'll break your fall."

He was right. So she didn't think. She just took a deep breath and let herself drop.

Max kept his word and let her fall onto him, nearly knocking him down. But despite the rough landing, she ended up in his arms and, miraculously, they both stayed on their feet.

Now on the ground, Kimberly looked around. Everything was gloriously still and not as dark as she might have hoped, but it was still much more shadowy than it would be in the morning when the sunlight came blasting through the windows near the ceiling. They'd picked a good time to escape.

Kimberly's stomach churned with nervousness as she and Max began to silently make their way around the heaps of glassware containers. A few tenuous moments later, they rounded a row of crates and then Kimberly spotted the door—the very same they'd come through yesterday afternoon. She grabbed Max's wrist and pointed. His eyes lit with relief and Kimberly thought, *We're actually getting out of here!*

And then a voice cut into her joy. "Well, what do we have here?"

Kimberly and Max both turned to find Carlo standing behind them.

"I don't know how you got out of that closet, but you sure as hell aren't getting out of this building alive."

Kimberly released a ragged, disbelieving sigh. A part of her wanted to cry, but another part of her quickly realized that he was alone. And what had she told Max? If they went up against only one person, they should separate. He'd practically forbidden it, but she didn't care. She had to trust her instincts now—she could see no other way.

She strode boldly toward Carlo without giving Max a glance. She only prayed he'd stay where he was. "Brandt," he snapped, but at least he didn't seem to be following her.

Oddly, Carlo took a step or two back, obviously confused by her approach. "What the hell..." he muttered. She thought for a moment that maybe he would make this easy, maybe she could just walk up and take his gun herself.

But then he pulled it from the back of his waistband, just as she'd known he would.

Instead of stopping, she kept moving toward him, which clearly confused him even more. "Hold still!" he said.

"Carlo," she purred, "you wouldn't hurt me, would you?"

He seemed unable to decide whether to hold the gun on Kimberly or on Max. He chose Max in the end, figuring him to be more adversarial, she guessed, but his eyes had gone soft at her seductive tone.

"Would you?" she whispered. Soon she was at his side, so close she could have reached up and kissed him, and she knew he was thinking the same thing.

"I...don't want to hurt you, Kimberly," he said. "You know that."

"Yes, I know that," she breathed, widening her eyes, meeting his gaze, and trying to figure out exactly how she could get the gun from him.

But then Max said, "Damn it, Brandt, get away from him."

Carlo swung his gaze back to Max, shouting, "Get your hands where I can see 'em."

Before Carlo could figure out what to do next, Kimberly spotted one of the heavy white pitchers they'd found yesterday, and she picked it up, crashing it on Carlo's head, hard. He crumpled to the ground before her, and Kimberly had just seen the alarm in Max's eyes when someone else behind her said, "Hold it right there!"

The words halted her in place and she turned to find three men with guns, all of them trained on her and Max. It felt as though her heart dropped to her stomach. She knew instantly that they'd come too far to give in now, and that their only chance lay in blatant and very risky defiance. The only other alternative was certain death.

She looked toward Max, her back to the gunmen. And she moved her lips to say, *Run*.

But Max just stood there, his eyes darting back and forth between Kimberly and the guys with the guns. She supposed he was determined to do something to save her, to treat her as the damsel in distress he seemed to think she was. But there was no time for that now. She had to force the issue. She mouthed the word to him again, this time with fire in her eyes. *Run!*

She bolted madly toward the door and Max joined her. Gunfire erupted behind them, bullets whizzing past her and people yelling. The danger was so thick she could taste it.

Suddenly, a sharp pain exploded in her hip and she looked down to see a bright red blot on her dress. She kept running in spite of it, although she felt strange and weak and heavy. And as they neared the door, she yelled at Max, "Tate, I've been shot!"

11

SHE'D BEEN SHOT? His Kimberly? No, it couldn't be. But a glance told Max it was true. Blood stained the left side of her dress.

"Can you keep going?"

"I think so."

They were at the door, Max pushing her through, running behind her. *I've got to get her safe, I've got to get her safe.*

He looked up and saw the street before him illuminated with eerie swirling lights—blue ones, on cop cars. They lined the front of the warehouse.

"Max! Kim!" The voice belonged to Frank, rising from somewhere amid the blue glow.

There was more gunfire behind them and Max tackled Kimberly, pushing her to the pavement, praying that it would all end soon, and that she wouldn't die. *Please don't let her die, God. Please.*

"THANKS AGAIN, Frank," Max said, clasping his friend's hand. "If you hadn't gotten that message and called the police in..."

"Hey, let's not think about that, huh?" Frank slapped him on the back and it helped Max lighten up a little. Still, Frank had really come through for them— a little late, but better than never. He and Kimberly were out of danger, and Carlo and all his buddies were on their way to jail.

And Kimberly, thought Max as he made his way through the chaos, had come through, too. She'd defied him by doing just the opposite of what he'd told her to when they'd confronted Carlo, but it had turned out to be a pretty good move. Still risky as hell, but it had worked. If those other guys hadn't come along, they'd have been home free.

A moment later, he kneeled next to her in an ambulance that was about to take her to the hospital. Thankfully, she'd sustained only a flesh wound, but she was wearing it like her very own Red Badge of Courage. "Can you believe I actually got shot, Max?" she said with a huge smile as an EMT cleaned and bandaged the scratches she'd gotten when Max tackled her.

He wanted to laugh and he wanted to cry. He'd never seen anyone so happy about getting shot. But he should have learned this weekend that if anyone could catch him off guard, it was Kimberly. He brushed back a strand of hair from her face.

"I wonder if I'll have a scar. I normally hate scars, but in this case, it might be kind of cool." She shifted her gaze to the young man currently pressing an adhesive bandage across her forehead. "Will I have one?"

"Probably," he said, his smile tinged with amusement.

Clearly pleased with his answer, she turned her gaze back to Max. "I wonder what it'll look like."

When the EMT was done, Max said, "Can we have a minute?"

The young man gave a friendly nod, then stepped out and closed the ambulance doors.

Alone with her for the first time since their escape, all Max's emotions came rushing back. He wanted to kill her. And he wanted to kiss her. He chose the second, taking her into his arms and giving her a long, deep kiss that he hoped shook her to her core as much as it shook him.

"I'm sorry, babe, about knocking you down. You didn't need that on top of a gunshot wound."

"You were only trying to protect me, Max. And besides, compared to taking a bullet, they're pretty minimal injuries." She was smiling again.

"Does it hurt?" he asked of the wound.

She nodded. "A little. But I feel...validated, you know?" Her eyes sparkled. "Like a real P.I."

He sighed. "You were already a real P.I., Kimberly."

She gazed up at him, quiet and thoughtful. "Really, Max? Do you truly feel that way?"

He nodded. "Completely, babe. And you're damn good at your job."

A small smile graced her face. "Thank you."

KIMBERLY LAY in the hospital bed, wanting to admire the bandages on her wound, but they were beneath the white gown she wore.

"Hey."

She looked up to find Max standing in the doorway bearing a vase of bright summer flowers. She was both happy and sad to see him. After a few hours apart, the very sight of him turned her to jelly, but she knew things would change now, that they'd go their separate ways.

"Hi," she said. "Pretty flowers."

"For a pretty lady," he said, setting them on the table next to the bed.

"Even now?" she asked, thinking of the scratches and scrapes on her forehead and chin.

"Even now," he said. "I'd go so far as to say always."

The words touched her, but for some reason, she played them off as teasing. "Always, huh? That's a pretty big step to take, Tate. Sure you're ready to go that far?"

"For you, babe," he teased her back, "I'd go anywhere."

Those words tugged at her heart, too, and she wished it wasn't all just playful banter.

"So tell me," she said, changing the subject, "what was the deal with Carlo? Who did he work for?"

"Turns out Dormer and Sons is a legitimate shipping business like you thought, or at least *partially* legitimate. Apparently, old man Dormer—the boss guy we had the displeasure of meeting—has had mob connections since he was young, but he didn't tie that part of his life in with his business until a couple of years ago when he quit turning much of a profit. His mob friends thought a shipping business would be a convenient way to smuggle stolen jewelry, so Dormer decided to give it a try. Apparently, the jewelry went to New York, where it was sold to stores and collectors from all over the world. The bulk of glassware that leaves the warehouse, though, is just that—glassware."

"Wow," she said. "So we nabbed a major crook."

Max smiled and gave her a short nod.

"What about Carlo in specific?" Kimberly asked. "Where does he fit in?"

"He's one of about a dozen low-level guys Dormer hired to do his dirty work. Got into the business when his father—a wealthy playboy type, also with a few mob connections—died without leaving him a penny. Carlo's mistake, though, was his fascination with tying seduction in with thievery. It made his crimes stand out from the rest. Which was where we entered the picture.

"But enough about cops and robbers for today," Max concluded. "How are you feeling?"

"Good," she said. "A little tired, but not bad under the circumstances."

"I could use some rest myself," Max replied. "But I wanted to stop by and check on you first."

That was sweet, she thought.

But sweet was not love.

She knew the longer he was there, the sadder she would be when he finally left. Because just as she'd thought the last time they'd parted three years ago, this would be for good. "Well, I'm fine," she said. "So you're...free to go."

Next to her, Max hesitated. She peered into those dark, beautiful eyes of his and saw a tiny hint of indecision, but not much. Not enough to count.

"One more thing, Brandt," he said.

"What's that?"

"I want to tell you that I meant it earlier when I said you really were a good P.I. And I want to tell you, too, that I...forgive you."

This took her aback a little. "Forgive me?"

"For the Carpenter case. For the whole job thing."

She took a deep breath and said those teasing words

again, but this time she meant them. "That's a pretty big step to take, Tate. Sure you're ready to go that far?"

He nodded. "Yeah. I am."

"Well...thank you, Max. That means a lot to me."

And it truly did, but Kimberly wanted so much more than that from him now. Yet the sad truth was, it just wasn't going to happen.

"You should go sleep," she managed to say.

Max gave a slight nod, then squeezed her hand in parting before walking out the door.

As a solitary tear rolled down Kimberly's cheek while she gazed at the empty doorway, she realized in a moment of startling clarity that she'd finally learned to read Max's eyes. And they'd just told her goodbye.

She might truly be tough inside, but where Max was concerned, she was as helpless as ever.

MAX WALKED down the crisp white hospital corridor, thinking of getting in his car and going home and climbing into bed for a week. It sounded so easy, so restful. So...*oddly empty*. Where had that thought come from?

When he really examined it, things started looking emptier and emptier with each step he took. After all, what was waiting for him at home? An empty condo. What waited at work? A job that, at the moment, seemed almost just as empty. It *all* suddenly seemed empty...*without her*.

Keep walking, he told himself as he went through the revolving door and out into the southern California heat toward the parking lot.

Why? another part of him answered back.

Because it's what you do, it's how you play your life. He kept moving.

But why? What are you running from?

After all, hadn't he forgiven her? Yes, he had. But this was more than that. This...was about sharing his life with somebody. Really sharing it. He wanted to, but it was still pretty scary at the same time. Being a P.I., putting yourself in constant dangerous...that was nothing compared to the real fear that haunted him now.

But if you keep walking, you'll never see her again. Never brush another strand of hair away from that pretty face. Never hear that sweet laughter. Never gaze on the seductive heat in her eyes.

"I can't live without her," he said out loud. He looked around, glad to see he was alone in the parking lot. And he turned to go back inside.

"I CAN'T LEAVE." He approached her bed. Was she crying?

"Why not?" she said through a sniffle. "Car won't start?"

"No, it's you, Kimberly."

"What about me?" She wiped at her eyes with a tissue.

"I love to argue with you," he said.

"What?"

"It's insane, I know, but I love it."

Kimberly simply stared at him, obviously waiting for him to say something that made sense. He wasn't doing very well so far. So much for being impetuous again, but he had to forge on because he only had one shot at making this right. "And I love to make love to you," he said.

She still looked baffled. He knew he was still doing a lousy job, but he'd never actually done this before. "So you're saying...what?" she asked.

Just tell her, he thought. "I'm saying that I love you." He shook his head, amazed at how easy that had been. "God, that felt good. To just say it. I've been afraid of the words, but suddenly I realized I've got nothing to lose...except you, if I don't tell you this. I've loved you for...a long time. It took this weekend to make me see it, accept it. I've missed you, Kimberly, and I don't want to let you get away again."

"You don't?"

"No, I don't." Then he took a deep breath and blurted out the next part. "Marry me."

"Huh?"

Okay, now she was making this difficult. "You heard me, Brandt. I want to marry you. I want to feel like I feel when I'm around you all the time, for the rest of my life."

"You do?" Her voice was trembling and the way she was looking at him was suddenly making him think that maybe, just maybe, spending their lives together wasn't such a new idea to her.

"I really do," he said. "Will you? Marry me, Kimberly?"

"Oh, Max. Yes!"

And then he was on the bed with her without really planning it, taking her into his arms, kissing her soft and warm and deep, and whispering, "This feels so nice," and then, "Jeez, am I hurting you?" when he remembered her wound.

But she only shook her head, laughing, that pretty laughter he'd been afraid he'd never hear again, that pretty laughter that had drawn him back here to this perfect moment.

Kimberly almost didn't believe it. It was too wonderful to be true. "Oh, Max," she breathed, "I've loved you for so long and I never thought you'd love me back."

"I always have, babe. I was just too stubborn to see it. But you made me see it this weekend."

She smiled, still enraptured, still partly in disbelief, as he looked into her eyes.

"You were so hot, so sexy, and so soft and smart and tough. You're every woman, Kimberly," he said, laughing. "What guy could want more than that?"

Kimberly sighed with joy, glad the tough part of her was for real, glad the soft part of her was still intact, and glad he loved all of her. She twined her arms around his neck and pulled him into another long, languid kiss as Max smoothly ran his hands up under her hospital gown.

"You don't have any panties on, Brandt."

She bit her lip coquettishly. "My partner ripped them off when we were having hot sex last night."

He raised his eyebrows at the reminder. "Any chance you're up for a repeat performance?"

Kimberly laughed. "I thought you were tired."

But Max was already off the bed and closing the door, then sliding the visitor's chair in front of it. Returning to the bed, he flashed a devilish grin. "Not *that* tired, babe."

Epilogue

"I NEED A WOMAN."

"You've got a beautiful one right there."

Frank pointed across his living room toward Kimberly in her bridal gown. He'd given her away at the ceremony and was now hosting the wedding reception.

Max smiled and took a moment to study her himself. After all, they'd only have one wedding day and she looked lovely in her flowing ivory dress.

That was why he hated to muddy the day with business. But just before he'd left for the church he'd gotten an urgent call from a client who needed some undercover work done. The job could wait until he and Kimberly returned from their honeymoon to Hawaii in two weeks, but he'd have to at least start making the arrangements before they left.

"It's for a job," Max said.

"What are the parameters?"

"The usual," Max replied. "Smart, good instincts, good acting abilities. And she needs to be attractive, too."

"Like I said, Max, you've got a beautiful woman right there."

Max watched Kimberly once again—she was dancing to a Leon Redbone song with Max's father. The sight brought a smile to his face, but he let it fade as he turned to Frank. "It's a dangerous job."

"She's a capable woman."

"The job calls for a guy, too," Max said.

"You're a capable guy."

"But I'm getting out of the field, remember?"

"What's going on over here?" Apparently, the dance with his dad had ended because Kimberly had just come up the steps to the foyer where the two men stood. She planted her hands on her hips. "You look way too worried for your wedding day, Max."

"It's like this," Frank said before Max could even begin to reply. "He's got a dangerous job lined up that he's afraid to let you take. Oh, and there'll be a male partner involved, too, and he's too jealous to let you work with anyone but him, but he refuses to do it himself because he wants to quit."

"How many times do I have to tell you, Frank?" Max said, exasperated. "I'm not quitting...I'm taking a step back."

"Quitting," Frank said.

"How dare you!" Kimberly interjected. "Whatever that job is, Max, I want it! And I want you to do it with me! Got it?"

Max tossed a glance at Frank. "There's that sassy side I told you about."

"I like it," Frank said.

"So," she said, "are we square on this? We're doing this together?"

Max tilted his head. "You remember what happened the last time we worked together, babe. I didn't handle it well. I let my emotions—"

"Get in the way," she finished for him. "Yes, I

know." Then she reached up and kissed him on the cheek. "But you're a good P.I., Tate. You'll learn."

He couldn't help smiling.

"So, do we have a deal? As soon as the honeymoon's over, we go to work together?"

Max sighed, then gazed into her eyes, today a stunning shade of emerald that sparkled when she smiled. "Oh, what the hell," he said. "Who wants to quit anyway?"

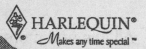

***Don't miss
an exciting opportunity
to save on the purchase of
Harlequin and Silhouette books!***

Buy any two Harlequin or
Silhouette books and save
$10.00 off future Harlequin
and Silhouette purchases

OR

buy any three
Harlequin or Silhouette books
and save **$20.00 off** future
Harlequin and Silhouette purchases.

***Watch for details
coming in October 2000!***

PHQ400

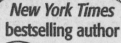

HARLEQUIN®
Temptation.

Buckhorn County, Kentucky, may not have any famous natural wonders, but it *does* have the unbeatable Buckhorn Brothers. Doctor, sheriff, heartthrob and vet—all different, all irresistible, all larger than life.

There isn't a woman in town who isn't in awe of at least one of them.

But somehow, they've managed to hang on to their bachelor status. Until now...

Lori Foster presents:

Sawyer
#786, On Sale June 2000

Morgan
#790, On Sale July 2000

Gabe
#794, On Sale August 2000

Jordan
#798, On Sale September 2000

The
BUCKHORN
BROTHERS

All gorgeous, all sexy, all single.
What a family!